Act Two
A Novel

All rights reserved. No part of this book may be reproduced, distributed, or transmitted in any form or by any means without the prior written permission of the copyright owner.

All characters appearing in this work are fictitious or products of the author's imagination. Any resemblance to real persons, living or dead, is purely coincidental.

Author photo by Luis Cordero.

Copyright © 2011 Brenda Ann Fraser

All rights reserved.

ISBN: 1466295767
ISBN-13: 9781466295766

Act Two
A Novel

Brenda Ann Fraser

Trish,
Developing a character that selflessly gives to others was my goal for Aimee. I hope you recognize her untiring persistance as traits you've shown me for years. I hope you enjoy reading this book as much as I did writing it!

L,
Brenda

DEDICATION

This book is dedicated to my Posse,
without whom my life would feel one-dimensional,
and I wouldn't be half the woman I am today.

An Ordinary Day

It's amazing how one night can change a life. Or, as it was in this case, change five lives. Okay, okay, I'll start at the beginning. I am blessed in life to have four wonderful girl friends. We are a group that gathered along the way, without a lot of rhyme or reason in what brought us together. We may not understand the glue that makes us stick. We just know we stick. And don't try to break us apart... Let me tell you about "the Posse".

Meet Regina. A long time ago, when I was a lowly freshman in college, there was this girl, you know the type. She sat up front, always raised her hand, and *always* had her homework done early. You could say she was the complete opposite of me. If I weren't so busy covering my envy by playing it cool, I'd have gotten to know her right away. It wasn't until Christmas break that we spent any time together. We were assigned to be partners on a project due right after the holidays. Since most students went home for the break, the cafeteria was closed when we met there to work. Regina showed up with 2 huge cups of Dunkin' Donuts coffee and all the appropriate condiments. She came with coffee! We've been BFFs ever since, long before that term was even invented.

After graduation, real life set in. I moved away from home and started a career on my own. After a failed startup that almost broke my spirit, I landed at a big computer manufacturing company. In an age when the majority of technical jobs were taken by men, I was thrilled to meet a couple other women. In time, we became great friends. Aimee is an early entrepreneur. She owned various businesses, worked a "real" job, and basically burned the candle at both ends. Susan was a New York City transplant. She's the cultivated one, the one who drags us to museums, makes us read books to better our minds, and taught us many things we never expected we'd be interested in.

Around this time, my little brother was finally grown up enough to get to college. There he met the woman of his dreams. Through their very, very... *very* long courtship, Lauren and I became dear friends, practically sisters. As a matter of fact, I told my brother at least a few times that if they ever broke up, I was keeping Lauren!

It didn't happen immediately, but over time, through life's joys and sorrows, my girlfriends met and we became a sisterhood. We have a bond that encourages us to take on challenges, push our limits and support each other. This story isn't about how we became the Posse. It's about where we go from here. Imagine the 'what if's', and 'why not's' of tomorrow. Let's move on to Act Two...

Chapter 1
One Door Closes

I woke up ready to face the day. I always felt good after a weekend with the girls. My boss called me first thing in the morning. As I walked to his office, I was wondering what customer crisis was about to derail my week. "Jules, as you know, the company isn't doing well and we need to make some cuts."

"Yeah, we talked about this. When's it happening?" Layoffs are always tough. The people who lose their jobs have their entire life turned upside down. For those left behind, it's like a death in the family. Guiltily, you think "thank God it wasn't me", but you know it could have been. For all you know, next time it will be.

"Jules, I hate to tell you this, but your job has been eliminated."

What? My job? But I worked with him to develop the list. He never even hinted I could be on the list. How could he get rid of me... How could I have not seen this coming? What am I going to do?

Wait a minute? Isn't this exactly what I wanted? I'm free to do whatever I want. What do I want to do? Maybe I should have felt a premonition Saturday when the posse talked about tomorrow being the first day of the rest of our lives. Bring it on!

I am 49 years old. Next year, it's the Big 5-0 for me. I'm an engineering manager in a high tech company and spend the majority of my days dealing with men. Men who have a wife at home to clean up after them and want me to do the same at work – not the same messes, but any undesirable task they don't want to do. Tasks I consider on par with putting their dirty clothes in the hamper or picking up for them after they eat. I often joke that I'm the highest paid babysitter/maid in New England. Maybe I'm ready to leave the high tech world for something completely new.

I've always defined myself by my relationships with others. When I met my husband Frankie, I defined myself as his girlfriend, then his wife. When our kids came along, I defined myself as their mom. Now that our youngest is well into his adulthood, I no longer give that role premier billing. I'm not needed at home like I was in the past and so I've been looking for fulfillment from work. Last weekend when I was talking with the girls and we toasted to "what if", I was scared. I was so secure in my daily grind. Even though my career didn't satisfy me as much as it could, I was comfortable. Am I ready to toss that all up in the air to see where it leads? I've never really been that brave. Maybe today's the day.

Today I got fired. Not exactly fired, laid off. I got out of bed this morning planning to figure out how to move on with my life. I wanted to get out of the professional rut I'm stuck in and start fresh. I never anticipated getting so much support on that goal from the company I've been loyal to for over thirteen years. With nine months severance pay and then unemployment, I can't complain. I am excited! I wouldn't be honest if I didn't admit my excitement is a bit tempered by my fear.

I head home to cry on Frankie's shoulder. When Frankie and I met in college, I loved that he was a bad boy. Even his name sounded 'bad' – Francisco. The attraction I felt didn't diminish when I found out he went by the nickname Frankie. Whenever my mood gets bleak, Frankie magically turns my energy positive. Whether I'm pissed or depressed, he can talk me around the emotions to start solving the problem. This time is different. He knows I'm not ready to start moving forward. I need to spend some time wallowing in my misery. I need the posse and Frankie quickly convinces me to give Aimee a call.

Aimee's a driven woman, never happy unless she's going a mile a minute. She has various degrees in technology and nutrition. It's an odd combination, but Aimee makes it work somehow. When the high tech bubble crumbled around her, Aimee left the industry and never looked back. She is working at a teaching hospital helping overweight people figure out the best way for them to lose weight. At long last she has a career she loves! Every pound a client loses puts a brighter smile on Aimee's face. Finding a career she could pour her love and passion into was a long road for her. Aimee was an only child, very close to both her parents. She grew up knowing she was loved and with the belief that she could do anything she set her mind to. We met a long time ago when I was newly married and she was an old hand at it. She threw my baby showers when my babies came along and taught me how to balance a career with a family. That was all so long ago.

Aimee got interested in healthy eating when her husband died unexpectedly from a heart attack. She wasn't able to help him fight the disease, but with enough education and her skills at making taboo subjects approachable, she could help others. Diet and exercise became her mantra. Aimee is never pushy or preachy about being healthy, which works well. She's lost enough weight in her past to earn creditability with her students, and loves junk food as much as the next person. She has learned the boundaries that need to be maintained for a healthy life and the art of teaching that to others. Interestingly, half the time we get together we are either testing new recipes or eating the results, the delicious and nutritious ones!

When I've messed up and need a cheerleader to get me going again, Aimee is always there for me. With Frankie's urging, I call to tell her the news. "Hallelujah! You are finally free of that place!" Aimee shouts. I can almost see the pom poms. "Isn't this exactly what you've been hoping for?" She's right. Unfortunately, when the road is wide open in front of you, it's hard to see anything but a maze. We decide to get everyone together. Lucky for us, Aimee has a beef stew simmering.

Regina comes from a big Italian family in East Boston. She's second generation off the boat. Regina is the only girl in her family, with lots of good looking, over protective brothers. Definitely the kind of girlfriend you want growing up! Her grandparents owned a bakery where we hung out and flirted with her brothers' friends who were always coming by looking for a handout. In our twenties, we lived together and enjoyed the freedom well-paying jobs allowed us. She married a guy who didn't turn out to be the man he pretended to be or the man she deserved. After many years of being the good wife, Regina grew tired. She couldn't keep up the façade of a happy marriage any longer and he wasn't willing or able to change. In true form, Regina stayed loyal until the end, waiting for their son to be old enough to handle the break up. Their son was nearly a grown man when they finally got divorced. It was time to get her life back and do something for herself. Aaron was very supportive and helped his mom transition from being part of a struggling marriage to being single again. Right now, Regina is busy getting ready for Aaron's graduation party. Next weekend, Regina is throwing a huge bash for Aaron, and the posse is helping every way we can. This is our tradition for each of our children when they graduate college. He is graduating magna cum laude and starting his career in the financial world. When Aaron was ten years old, he marveled at the gas station attendant and his wad of bills. I suspected that he would end up managing money some day, and I was right! I really hate to bug Regina when she has so much else on her mind, but she'd kill me if I didn't include her. She always manages to make time for us when the need arises.

I don't even know if Susan is in the country. She's been traveling so much since she got promoted to Vice President of Engineering at her company that I can never seem to remember which continent she's on. Let me give her a call. Susan has been single all her life. Maybe it would be more accurate to say that Susan is married to her career and doesn't have time for romance. To fill the void the rest of us filled with our kids, Susan began volunteering. She is the managing director of the Alliance House, a shelter in Boston for abused and homeless women. The programs she's developed are heavily focused on career and life coaching. She refocuses these women from feeling sorry for themselves to feeling empowered. I think that's a winning combination. Based on the success rate of those leaving her shelter to live on their own, I'm certain they do too!

Susan has two brothers and two sisters, but none of them live around here. Her parents live here, and she spends a lot of time with them. They are getting old and she's helps them out as much as they let her. Susan has doted on her nieces and nephews and spent countless hours with our kids. She is so funny with kids. If you sit back and watch, you can see her trying to debug them, trying to get into their little minds to see what makes them tick. Why did they ask that? What made them do that? Why won't they stop asking why? Still, if you look closely, you can see the sadness she feels that no one has ever called her "Mom".

Susan is a pragmatic, driven and very giving person. She pushes herself hard and pushes everyone around her just as hard. She's been trying to get me to leave my job for at least five years. She even redesigned my resume to make me highly marketable. She sent a job opportunity my way that I almost landed about a year ago. She'll be thrilled to hear my news.

When I call Lauren, I hope her husband doesn't answer. Lauren is married to my little brother, Shamus. We giggle sometimes when she shares too much about her happy marriage, especially if I begin to picture that she's talking about my brother. There are times I need my girlfriend, not my brother. Shamus understands, mostly. He and I were best friends growing up but sometimes he gets jealous and feels like he's been replaced by Lauren. I guess I feel that way too sometimes, like Lauren's replaced me with Shamus. Regardless, I am thrilled we've managed to build a strong relationship that has room enough for all three of us.

Lauren and Shamus are the happiest married couple I know. They met in college and dated forever before deciding to get married. They both have successful careers and share the load of parenting equally. Their twins are the youngest of our kids. Russell and Carter are seniors in high school this year. I fully expect Lauren and Shamus to retire after the boys finish college. They've been dreaming for years of getting out of this rat race and seeing the world.

I'm sure they are busy tonight, but right now, I need them all. Some to dole out hugs, some to sternly get me focused on a productive path, all to give me the that wonderful unconditional support and encouragement that I can't get anywhere else. Oh, and Regina to bring the chocolate cake!

৵৽

When I think about the decades that comprise my career, I am discouraged to admit I have never had a really good boss. Besides a single semester in college, I never had a boss who is a good mentor or motivational leader. I don't think my standards are even that high. Lauren raves about her boss Phil. She met him when she was two years out of college. He encouraged her to push herself and take risks that were beyond her comfort zone. Every time she succeeded, he was the first to applaud and passed all the glory to her. She was never afraid to take on difficult projects under him, and the more she learned, the higher her corporate growth. When Phil moved on to another company, he took Lauren with him, repeatedly. Four companies later, they are still working together as a very successful team. Susan, Regina and Aimee all had similar relationships with bosses. I've had my share of bosses through the years. None of them were technical enough to understand the details of our products. That didn't stop any of them from being so motivated to climb the corporate ladder that they would step on whoever they could to reach the next rung. More often than I care to count, I felt like I was the woman left doing the work for the man personifying the Peter Principal! I also have a loyalty problem. In over 25 years, I've only worked for three companies. Crazy!

"Congratulations Jules! I'm so happy for you!" Susan greeted me as she came through the door. "You are finally free of that place. Free of that boss. You must be so excited to move on." How do I explain the excitement is tempered with shock, embarrassment and good old fashioned anger? I'm sure she knows the pool of emotions I'm swimming in. It wasn't that long ago it happened to her. In the end, it all worked out well for her. She got a summer off and a new job she loves! As Aimee filled our glasses, she said "we are just waiting for Lauren before we make the toast. Look, here she is. Quick, now let's toast to Jules and her new beginnings!"

As usual, we dig into the food, the wine and the chatting. We all talk at once, then repeat our sagas until everyone's heard everything and we have a lull. That's when I remember – Donald Trump. Without thinking too much about it, I blurt out "I want to work for Donald Trump! He isn't climbing any corporate ladder, he's already reached the top. I know you've seen The Apprentice, he spends weeks mentoring candidates that don't even work for him, most of who never will. That's what I want! I want to be on The Apprentice!" Sure, fine. I'll reset my expectations. I'll update my resume and start looking for something more realistic. It should probably be local too. As a side task, I'm going to figure out how to apply to The Apprentice. Why not!

By the time the cake is served and the wine is gone, we start thinking about heading home. It's been a long day. I'll figure out where to start after a good night sleep.

ಹೊಡ

Regina's son Aaron, my Godson, is graduating from Suffolk University with a Masters in Finance. We are all so proud of him. The Posse is helping Regina with his party and it's going to be a blow-out! In a week, Aaron will be a Fraud Prevention Analyst at Boston Private Bank and Trust. Today we are celebrating his success at school and his future! Sharing the successes of our lives makes weathering the sorrows that much easier. This is a hard earned success! Regina has been on her own for seven years, six of which Aaron spent in college. With his career set to begin in the city, he'll still be just a stone's throw away from his mom. She's so happy he took this job and not one of the others he was offered out of state.

There are lots of friends and family at the party and Aaron is thrilled to be the center of attention. He's been in school a long time. Since he decided to get his Master's degree directly after his Bachelor's degree, his friends all graduated a couple years ago. Some have moved away, and we haven't seen them since high school. Aaron has grown into such a handsome man, and smart! When we joke that he'll support us all one day, Aaron cringes a bit. He's afraid that threat might one day come to fruition.

As the party winds down, Regina tells me that come Monday, she'll be dedicating 100% of her energy on me. She's going to help me figure out the rest of my life. When Regina dedicates 100% of her effort to any one thing, you better watch out! That girl has more energy than anyone else I know.

༄༅

Sipping her morning tea, Aimee glances at the winning numbers for the lottery. Why can't it be us? Sure, we've won a few hundred dollars, but why can't we win the big one? Aimee's been playing the same numbers for the Posse for twenty years. The numbers are somehow derived from our birthdays, when we met, how many children we have, or some mathematical magic. After all these years, we aren't really even sure how she came up with them, we just know one of these days those numbers have to hit!

Every time the jackpot gets really big or one of us gets really down, we fantasize about what we'd do if we won. When we were younger, still unsure of our life choices, we said we'd all buy houses on the same cul-de-sac. "Like that show in the '80s, remember?" No one watched that show except Aimee, but we all went along with it. We'd share dinner most nights, we'd have a community garden and own one lawn mower. As we got a little older, we cared less about the lawn mower and looked forward to sharing the pool boy, though none of us cared if we had a pool or not. Now when we talk about it, our dreams are less concrete. We want to provide for our kids, and grandkids. We want to go back to school. We want to get out of the rat race. Wow, without a job, it's a little like I won the lottery... Albeit without the millions...

Since Aimee knows our numbers by heart, she realizes right away that another week will go by without us collecting a windfall. True to the optimist she is, she starts thinking about our chances next week before she even turns the page of the newspaper.

One of the simple pleasures in Regina's life is that she works in Boston, a short bus ride from her home. At various times, she has worked closer to home but nothing compares to being able to take a brisk walk in the city at lunch time. Regina is rejuvenated every day by the sights and sounds of the bustling city. The sunshine and flowers are great, but nothing gets her juices going better than having her lunch in the park with all those gorgeous men walking past. Okay, having one join her on the bench to share the hour and a bit of small talk is better, definitely better! Today is one of those Indian Summer days where the bright sunshine is glittering off the water. Where despite the undercurrent of chill in the air, people are tossing Frisbees and playing with their babies in the park. It's the kind of weather that begs for strangers to strike up conversation and maybe spark something more. Regina is hopeful. She's always hopeful.

"Can you believe it's the middle of November?" Regina asks the man who sat down close by and was unwrapping a meatball sub dripping with sauce and cheese. He looks up from the sandwich and replies "it seems like just yesterday I was watching the Red Sox opening game."

Regina continues the banter, able to hold her own with sports talk about any of the Boston teams. If you want to know who traded whom and how close the local teams are to the championships, Regina's your girl. Before long, time runs out and Regina needs to get back to work. As she heads back, she smiles. Life is good.

When she gets home, there's a call on her machine from Aaron. "Mom, why don't you ever keep your cell phone turned on? I need to talk to you. I have good news!" At this, Regina decides to put the tea pot on before calling her son back. On the second ring, Aaron answered, "Mom, I met a girl. I think she's the one." Regina chuckles gently and says "Oh Aaron, you have always been so quick to fall in love." And just as quick to fall out of love. Regina is smart enough not to verbalize her second sentiment. "This is different Mom. Really. Just wait until you meet Sarah."

The next Sunday, Aaron brought Sarah to meet Regina. Aaron isn't surprised to find the whole Posse there, but Sarah wasn't expecting us. How intimidating we must be for a young girl! I'm happy to report that she survived our scrutiny. She said Aaron told her all about us. She hoped one day to have a group of friends as supportive and understanding as we were for each other and our entire extended families. Of course we loved her right away. Just as Aaron had.

"Sarah, how did you and Aaron meet?" Lauren asked when we were just sitting down with our first cups of coffee. "I'm the property manager of his building. They are expanding their space and I was there reviewing the layout with the architect. Aaron came in to discuss their need for many small soundproof offices. I thought the idea was crazy until I heard him explain the need to discuss confidential financial matters with remote clients via skype. Then it made perfect sense." We all smiled as she spoke. Sarah asked "What did I say that's so funny?" Could we tell her? Her words, that smile, those eyes, they were all shouting "this time it's for real". One look at Aaron and you see his every cell is shouting the same thing. I'm predicting there will be fireworks here!

Sarah offered to help us clean up and we took her up on it. We wanted to be sure she was good enough for our Aaron. After an hour of dishes and chit-chat, we all agree she is! Her loyalty to Aaron was already strong and when we started telling stories of the little boy who lined up his Matchbox cars by color and slept with a tattered Ernie doll until he hit puberty, she quickly jumped to his defense saying that only proves how orderly and sensitive he is. I have a good feeling about this one.

Regina isn't one for self pity, but come Monday morning, she was feeling a little bit down. Her baby boy is moving on, growing away. "Why am I feeling sorry for myself? Did I expect Aaron to stay single forever, spending all his free time with me? That's not what I want. I want him to be happy and I want him to have love in his life!" With that, Regina got herself up and out. What better way to boost her energy than a long, hard workout at the gym? If she recalled from previous early morning workouts, the scenery isn't bad either.

ஒஒ

Susan just called. Her mom had another spell. After being checked out at the local hospital, they insisted she spend a few days in a rehab center. Again. "It's so hard to see

Mom like this. She needs help but is too stubborn to accept it. That's when she overexerts herself, falls and gets hurt. She saw this happen with Nana. Why can't she remember that and learn from it? I need to get her to let me help her so she doesn't get worn out and hurt herself." I'm so sorry for Susan, but can't help picturing twenty years from now when someone is saying the same thing about her. "I know it's hard Susan, but you're threatening her independence. That's all she has left. That's why she's fighting you so hard. You just can't use logic here. This is too emotional for logic."

Susan tells us that in high school she was awful to her parents. She says she was irrational, irresponsible and just plain mean. None of us can imagine it. First of all, Susan is the most logical, systematic person I know. She makes no decisions before carefully weighing all her options. Second, nothing ruffles her. When a crisis hits, she goes full force into solution mode, even before the flames have died down. Last but not least, mean? Not the Susan I know. Honest, brutally honest, okay. But never mean!

Susan detailed the chores her mother does every day. I can't imagine cooking a meal from scratch every day, but her Mom does it. If it weren't for the microwave and take-out menus, Frankie and I would never eat.

Susan decided the Posse would have brunch at her parents' house on Saturday. While we take turns distracting her mom with tantalizing storytelling, we'll also clean the house, do the laundry and bake a couple casseroles to reheat during the week. That will lift her burden without her even noticing we did anything. A perfectly constructed plan.

༻৽༺

The posse got together for coffee at the Daily Paper, our favorite neighborhood diner. We love it when Kristin is working. She's quick with the coffee refills and knows we'll tip well. We never feel rushed to leave, even when they are busy.

"I need to get motivated to move on with my life. Getting laid off was a blessing, but I still haven't decided what to try next. Honestly, I need to see if there is any way I could get a job with Donald Trump". As I expected, the girls glare at me. Nearly in unison, they start blurting "Are you crazy?", "That guy's a jerk", "Be careful what you wish for". I know they're probably right, but I've always thought working for him would be awesome. I am certain he wouldn't pussy foot around, or manipulate you for the sake of getting you to see his way, and then take credit for every single thing you do. He couldn't possibly have time for that. He would have to be direct and not mince words, be upfront and not waste valuable time on manipulation, and appreciate those of us working for him. Listen to me "those of us working for him", like I already have the job. But what if...

I spend the night Googling past episodes of The Apprentice to see what's happened to earlier winners of the show. Most no longer work for Donald but that doesn't mean anything. Unfortunately they aren't currently casting for next season. I better come up with a Plan B.

Over the past 10 years, I decided if I ever had the choice, I'd leave high tech for good. There is no time like the present. I have a business degree, maybe it's time to put that to good use. Maybe Susan could use my help at the Alliance House.

I dropped by the shelter the next day to see if there was anything I could help with. After discussing it with Susan, we decide I could start a Resume Writing Workshop for the women living there. I would put a program together, then trial it at Alliance House. If I'm successful there, I can market the program to other shelters. It's great to have an idea, and something to keep me busy while everyone else is working.

Before I knew it, the holidays were here. Unlike every other year, I was not overwhelmed with a work schedule that curtailed my free time. I loved having the time to attend every party and event I was invited to attend. In the past, deadlines at work kept me from celebrating the holidays in grand style, forcing me to carefully select who to visit and where to spend my creative energy. This year is different! I have all the time in the world, and Christmas music playing in the stores brings such joy to my heart, even if it's only November 2nd! I decided to call each of my kids and set up time to take my grandchildren for some individual loving. Time for Grammy to spoil them and give their parents some quality time together. While I'm with the grandchildren, we'll pick out a perfect present for their parents. This will be such fun! I'll help the younger kids make a present, but I'll take the older ones shopping. I've learned the hard way that preteen boys do not like to make their parents anything, no matter how cool I think it is! That should fill up every weekend in November for me.

Between entertaining the grandkids and holiday baking, I have little time left to worry about a job. Somehow I manage to find the time to get my resume ready with a slant towards a business audience. While at home snuggling with Frankie on Christmas Eve, we talk in earnest about my career. We decide that I don't have to earn anything near what I was making. As a matter of fact, if I didn't want to go back to work at all, that would be fine. We'd have to downsize a little bit, but nothing drastic. What a gift! The freedom to do what I want. Forever.

Chapter 2
Midlife Crisis

"If I have to deal with that... that... person again, I'll scream!" Aimee has the patience of a saint, but the hospital administration was driving her crazy. Currently almost half her week is spent doing paperwork. "I see a client for 30 minutes and then I have to dictate my notes, submit them for transcription, get back the typed version, proof read it and then resubmit it with corrections. After all that, then I have to submit the insurance paperwork." When she changed careers, she was looking forward to helping as many people a possible. She didn't realize the number of patients she could see would be so low because of the paperwork involved. Since she works at a teaching hospital, there is so much more "cover your ass" paper work, and quite frankly, Aimee is sick of it.

I had an idea, and I had the time to help her realize it. "Aimee, I know it's crazy, but why don't you go out on your own? Quit that place. Work for yourself so you can streamline the process. Spend more time helping people and less time filling out paperwork in triplicate." Judging by the look on her face, I'd say she likes the idea.

Aimee knows a few dieticians with private practices. If she could get them to talk to me for a few hours about running the business end of things, I could write a business plan that Aimee could use. I can't imagine it would take a lot of money upfront. What she'd really need is a way to get patients. There must be a way for doctors to recommend her when they refer a patient to a nutritionist. How hard could it be?

Suddenly I find I'm pretty busy for an unemployed woman. Between helping women at the Alliance House and working with Aimee on ways to start a business, I'm having a blast! I feel respected and appreciated. My business education is being used and I'm being challenged. Every day I'm learning something new. It's great!

Frankie's thrilled because there's a new spark in my life. The stress of the old job is completely gone. I'm energized and he's enjoying that energy as the night winds down and we're heading to bed.

In the doldrums of winter long after Christmas, but way before Memorial Day, Lauren and I were chatting about the twins. It's hard to believe they are almost through high school. It's been fun watching them grow up, from babies that seemed identical to young men who couldn't be more different.

"Russell has always loved skiing, but he's really good doing stunts on the half pipe. He is fascinated with Shaun White and the Olympics. I know it's a pipe dream – pardon the pun – but I wonder if we should let him try. He could take a year off before college and see if he can make the team. He wins every competition he's in, even the Junior Olympics and he's being pursued by some major Ski Board manufacturer to endorse their products." Both Lauren and Shamus were athletic through college, and both still regularly go to the gym. They raised the twins to be healthy and fit, always pursuing athletics over sedentary activities. If I'm hearing her straight, she's talking about the Olympics. We all love Russell, think he's the greatest! I can't help but wonder, is he really that good? If professionals think he is, who am I to doubt it?

"Lauren, that's a great idea! I think you should encourage him. Wouldn't it be amazing if he made the team? What an experience. Win or lose, you can never take that experience away from him." I want to go out and have t-shirts printed today 'Russell in 2014'! Where are the next winter Olympics anyway?" Lauren and Shamus have always been so supportive of the twins, giving them the freedom and opportunity to discover their own passions. Skiing has always been a family favorite and when Russell showed an interest shortly after he mastered walking, Shamus was overjoyed. They were both eager to see how his interest could flourish into a talent and possibly a career.

Carter enjoyed skiing, but was not overly interested. From the time he was a little boy, his passion was politics. He would toddle next door where their neighbor held rallies for local candidates. He moved from the "why?" stage of childhood into a questioning stage of adolescence. He has a quick mind that could seriously challenge the brightest political agendas. While Shamus and Russell traveled the competition circuit, Lauren and Carter attended political fundraisers, speeches and rallies. They were a busy crew.

From what Lauren is saying, we could all be going to the Olympics in two years! I need to find out where the games will be.

※

Susan just got back from another whirlwind trip abroad. She must be exhausted from all the travel she's doing. I know her career aspirations have always been VP of Engineering, but does she really want to be giving so much to her career at this point in her life? Her parents aren't getting any younger and she's riddled with guilt whenever she leaves town for very long. She knows we'll help out with anything they need, but she doesn't like putting that burden on us. She thinks of us like family, until she needs something. Then she wants to shoulder the entire burden herself. When she could the help the most, she won't let us in, even after all these years.

To add to Susan's stress, one of her favorite women at Alliance House is back. She's been an on-again, off-again resident, living with an abusive boyfriend and her little boy from another man. The guy gets drunk and hits her. She's willing to live with that, but when he goes after the boy, she leaves him. Until he begs her to come back and promises it will never happen again. "This time her son got beat up pretty bad. She swears she'll never go back. I've heard it before but I think it's different this time. Also there's bad news." As if this wasn't bad enough I thought. "She was diagnosed with cancer. It's lung cancer. She's prepared to fight, but is rightfully worried about her son."

"Can you tell me their names?" I asked. Susan has always been diligent about the residents' privacy but I got the impression we'd be talking a lot about these two. It would be a lot simpler to talk about them if we used their names. Now that I'm working at Alliance House a couple of days a week, I'm bound to figure it out.

"Sure, they are Jenny and her son Todd." Finally, I can put names to these people. I don't remember meeting them, but for now I can put names to the story. So far, while helping women with their resumes at Alliance House, I haven't met Jenny. She never seemed to be in residence while I was there. Maybe now I'll finally get to meet her. Maybe I can help her look forward to a future and encourage her in the fight for her life.

As I was heading home later that night, Susan planned to work on some paperwork for Alliance House. Tomorrow she was heading to her parent's house to pay their bills, do some food shopping and prepare meals for the week. I worry about her. She doesn't have the ability to turn it all off and relax. She's driving herself too hard. Even when the rest of my day is chaotic and I find myself frazzled, I always come home to Frankie. That slow smile at the end of the day never fails to warm my heart and quiet my soul.

৺৶

"Have you talked to your brother today?" I always know it's bad when Lauren calls Shamus "your brother". It doesn't happen often, but there's always a story about how he's taken up residence in the doghouse following that kind of reference. "No, I haven't. What's up?"

Turns out Shamus's company is expanding its presence in Germany and he was offered a one year position managing the building of the facility, hiring much of the staff and turning up operations. It's a wonderful opportunity and he's thrilled! The offer is such a vote of confidence from the owners and it comes with both a huge increase in responsibility and a comparable increase in pay. It would be a great step in enabling them to realize their dream of retiring when the twins finish college.

Of course, if Russell goes to the Olympics in 2014, his college will be delayed by a few years. An increase in pay will ensure they won't have to let that sideline their retirement dreams. What would Lauren do while Shamus went to Germany? If she stayed here, they could afford to visit often. Would that put too much of a strain on their marriage? Any other time and they'd have packed up the entire family and made it a big adventure. Carter is starting college in the fall and will live on campus. He will be self-sufficient and probably won't mind having his parents on a different continent. On the other hand, this will be Russell's only opportunity to qualify for the Olympics. He will need Shamus and Lauren's guidance to keep him focused on the prize and help him make the best choices. Picking their marriage over their careers has always been a simple choice. Likewise, the choice of their children over their careers has also been an easy one. The trouble is, this is a once in a lifetime opportunity for Shamus. He has dedicated so much of his life to his family, passing up career opportunities to ensure his availability to Lauren and the twins. He never regretted his decisions, but this time he really wants it. He wants to figure out some way they can all get what they want, and need, over the next year and come out stronger for the experience.

Lauren is beside herself with worry. She doesn't know what she wants. She can't decide what's best for everyone and is terrified she will let her desire to spend every day with the man she loves override the need for him to have this chance.

༄༅

I spent the day at Alliance House today giving my resume writing workshop. It was heartwarming talking to these women who are at first so down on themselves and seeing them come to life with pride when they begin to realize that they do have skills! With help phrasing their experiences to give them a business slant, these skills will truly be marketable. I wasn't sure who was more excited about the outcome, them or me! I worked with four women today. There are between 25 and 30 women at the shelter at any time and different women cycle in and out all the time. It will take a long time to get through everyone, but I am determined. I think I'll also develop an interviewing skills class. Also, I want to collect a bunch of career wear clothes. I'm sure my friends have closets full of clothes they no longer wear. What better group to donate them to?

When I get home, I'm exhausted. Frankie is waiting for me with a glass of wine and a back rub. What would I ever do without him? "Marie called. She just saw on Facebook that you aren't planning to look for a job 'at this time'. She is really mad that you still treat her like a child and don't tell her about your life."

Oh, I should have called her. I get so wrapped up in my own life that I forget to call her. I know she isn't a child anymore, but she'll always be my little girl. Maybe I can sweet-talk her into helping at the Alliance House. These women are closer to Marie's age than mine. I bet seeing a successful, happily married young woman would be inspiring to them. I settle into my favorite chair and pick up the phone. "Hi Marie. I'm sorry I didn't call you earlier…"

After a long chat, the likes of which only a mother and daughter can have, we promise to talk more often and say our goodbyes. "Well, I think she still loves me. At least she loves me enough to talk to her friends about coming to a clothes drive for the shelter. They will have outfits so much more appropriate than what the Posse will have, we are such old hags." As expected, Frankie immediately jumped to the defense of the Posse. "None of you are old hags. Especially not you." Flattery will get him whatever he wants!

In what seems like a blink of an eye, winter thaws and spring is in the air. It's been nearly a year since I lost my job. In that year, I have helped unfortunate women gain the confidence to break out of the cycle of abuse, secure employment and stand strong on their own two feet. In all my years toiling away in middle management, I never felt this much job satisfaction. I never felt that what I was doing made a difference. Now I do. I need to figure out how to channel this into a business that can grow beyond what a single person can do. I need a business plan.

Nearly as often as I was at the Alliance House, Susan was there with Jenny and Todd. Because of her illness, Jenny was allowed to stay at the shelter indefinitely. Since she wasn't well enough to go out on her own, exceptions were made so she wouldn't be forced back into the abusive living arrangement she came from. There is a school nearby that Todd attends and Susan has been working with him to be sure his homework is done properly each day.

"Todd is such a smart kid and he's been dealt such a tough hand. He's so young. I'm amazed he isn't bitter or jaded by the world already." Susan didn't usually warm up to children and her insight surprised me. I'm used to seeing compassion from Susan, just not typically directed toward kids.

"Jenny did such a good job shielding him from the abuse her boyfriend gave her. She really works hard to show him the world is a wondrous place, full of interesting people and limitless opportunity. He's so curious about everything. It's sad he's experienced so much pain at such a young age. It's even sadder that I don't expect that to stop for him any time soon."

Between Alliance House, her parents and travel for work, Susan is exhausted. She needs to find a way to slow down. Of course there is no discussing this with Susan. I've known her for nearly thirty years, and if there's one thing I know, it's that there is no talking Susan into doing something she doesn't want to do. I'm exhausted just looking at her.

ත්‍රෝ

Since we are all such good cooks and love experimenting with recipes, most Friday nights the Posse gets together to stay in for dinner and a movie. We take turns cooking and picking a movie, often sending friendly jabs at each other with our selections. If I want to poke Regina, I put raisins in dessert. If Aimee wants to poke at me, she picks a 'blood and guts' movie. You can always tell who the victim is by what's for dinner or what we watch. Half the fun is guessing who's sending the message to whom. Shamus and Frankie sometimes join us, but they pick their own movie or go play video games. Boys!

This week, it less about our selections for dinner and more about getting to the bottom of what's eating Regina. Since Aaron left for college, Regina has had lots of time on her hands. She had no trouble finding interesting things to keep her entertained. Recently, that changed. She began burying herself in her work. This was never her style and the Posse wouldn't stand for it. "What's up with you? You've never spent so much time at the office", I asked after the guys went off to play some Battlefield 3. We all noticed the change in her hours. Usually an increase in hours came with the stress of a looming deadline, but she hasn't mentioned any killer project.

Regina paused a minute, not sure if she should tell us the truth or come up with a story. At last she decided to go with the truth. She knew we'd have pulled it out of her eventually. "Since my boss retired, there has been a lot of jockeying for position. I never wanted to get involved with office politics, so I've always stayed below the radar. Anyway, we have new management in place and they are forming a consultant group. This group would be responsible for reviewing the software architecture of all products being developed. I really want to be part of this team. In the past, I've stayed so low key that many of the decision makers don't know my work. I need to be more visible to this new management team to get noticed."

We were all surprised. Ever since Regina became a mom, her career has been secondary. She has always done an excellent job, but she has never pursued promotion. I guess now that Aaron is out of college and beginning a career of his own, she's ready to take on more.

Susan immediately wants to know if there will be a lot of travel with this position. We give her such a hard time about being gone so much. I think Susan would like company in the harassed group. "Yes, there will be a lot of travel. Most of it will be in the country, but occasionally to our locations in Hong Kong and Italy." Quickly we have murmurs of good luck and other accolades. Finally Lauren raises her glass "To Regina getting a promotion and our next vacation to Hong Kong or Italy!" Here, Here!

It's been three years since Aimee began counseling at the Weight Center. As her pride continues to grow with each success, her impatience grows with the bureaucracy of the medical community. "Why do they have to charge so much for patients to take this program? It's ridiculous. Think of all the money insurance companies will save if people are healthier. If they would just look at our records they would see we have proven year after year that this program works." It's the same fight you hear over and over. Insurance companies will pay for patients to have open heart surgery but won't pay for nutrition counseling to teach them how to eat properly so they don't wind up right back in surgery.

It's a good reason to vote for socialized medicine. Of course Aimee doesn't really believe that, but she feels strongly that if you want to learn and are willing to put the effort in, you shouldn't be stopped due to lack of money. I think higher education should be free under the same conditions. Let people go to school for a long as they can continue to get good grades for free or very nearly free. What Aimee is providing at the hospital is the same thing, education that in the long run can both save your life, and save the insurance companies money.

Since the program offered through the hospital costs so much money and insurance doesn't cover it, Aimee is trying to find a loophole in her contract that would allow her to offer a similar course on her own time. So far, it looks like everything she does related to the course is property of the hospital. Since she needs this job, she'll have to wait until she finds a bullet proof way to provide counseling to people in need without risking her job.

Aimee and I spent the evening reviewing her contract as well as her certifications with the insurance boards. There has to be an affordable way she can bring this service to people. We just have to look harder. By midnight, we were bleary eyed and depressed, and unfortunately no closer to finding a solution. "Let's break for tonight" I say after stifling a yawn. I know Frankie is home waiting for me, and I could use a neck rub right about now.

Chapter 3
Summer of Discontent

As summer approaches, we all groan about training. Every year, we all walk in the Avon Breast Cancer Walk. The tradition began nearly two decades ago with Aimee walking alone and the Posse supporting her. We'd hire a masseuse and provide a filling carb-laden dinner and comfortable bed after her walk. As the years went on, the rest of us started volunteering to help run the event. Now we all walk it. As we begin the first step of the 39-mile walk, we toast our good fortune that not one of us has been burdened with breast cancer. We support the cause like a badge of courage, praying that our dedication will spare us and those we love. So far, it's working!

On the even years, we walk in Boston. In the odd years we make a vacation out of it and go walk somewhere we'd like to visit. Our favorite vacation walk so far was Washington DC. Maybe because it was our first outside of Boston, or maybe because Aimee's son lives there and showed us around "local style", who can tell? This year we are going to Santa Barbara. I've never been there. This should be exciting! We are all excited about walking in California. According to that song, it never rains in California. As we experienced a long time ago, there is nothing worse than walking 39 miles in the rain!

We are flying out on Tuesday and the walk is Saturday and Sunday. That should give us plenty of time to get acclimated. I wonder how hilly Santa Barbara is...

Since I haven't been working, getting into a training routine has been really hard. Even though it seems like I should have more time to train, I've actually had less time. Don't ask me how, it just happens that way. Aimee needs to get her whip cracking. We should be walking 15 miles on the weekends already, and we haven't started yet.

※

This afternoon over coffee, Lauren was telling me that they are seriously considering all the changes their family is facing. They have so many options to choose from and each of the options could lead their family down a different path. If it were five years ago, they would have jumped at the opportunity to move to Germany for a year. The kids would have adjusted, and Lauren and Shamus would have loved it.

Lauren discussed the opportunity with her boss. "Phil reminded me that our company offers sabbaticals that I have never taken. Every five years, we are given a six month leave to pursue whatever we want. Since I didn't take one after I completed five years of service, I could take a double one now. That means I could leave my job for a year, and be guaranteed my position back when I return." Sabbaticals were quite common in the late 1980s and early 1990s but I don't know any company other than Lauren's that still offer them. It must be because it's a California based company. They are so much more laid back than East Coast organizations.

Carter will be heading to college in the fall, but Russell hasn't figured out what he's going to do after high school graduation. After thinking about the options, I asked "can you really consider going to Germany for a year when the twins are just settling into school?" It isn't like them to leave settling in to chance. They know the Posse will be there and we'll tend to Carter and Russell like they are our own, but it isn't the same as having your parents ushering you into this first phase of adulthood.

"I wouldn't go to Germany. Shamus would go to Germany alone. Carter would start his freshman year at Yale University. That leaves Russell and I. I would take Russell to the Olympic qualification circuit." Wow! I almost fell out of my seat. I am shocked they are considering separating the family. I understand it's only for a year, but that could feel like forever. There are a couple competitions in Europe that Shamus could join them for, but that's it. They haven't decided yet, but need to within the next two weeks. Did I say Wow!

I noticed Regina settled back to her normal work schedule, which must mean she is no longer trying for the promotion. "What happen to the career aspirations?" Lauren asked while we were waiting for a table at our favorite pizza shop. Regina typically worked from 6:30 am until 3:30 in the afternoon. We were all jealous of her quitting time, but not so envious of starting work before the world woke up.

"I got selected for Grand Jury duty. I have to go to court four days a week for six months to hear cases. I will only be at work on Fridays. They wouldn't promote me and then put it on hold for six months. Since it's unlikely I'll be considered, there is no need to impress anyone." We were all disappointed for the lost opportunity, but excited about the Grand Jury.

In two weeks, Regina will be forgoing her 6:30 am start for a casual 8:30 start time. Her 3:30 end time will only be increased to 4:00. She will be in downtown Boston and able to have her morning coffee and lunch breaks perusing an entirely new landscape of men. If I know Regina, she is looking forward to the change of scenery!

As an added bonus, Aaron's office is around the corner from the court house so they'll plan to get together occasionally for breakfast. Hopefully Sarah will join them. Aaron and she are getting quite serious. I think we'll be planning a wedding soon. It will be nice for Regina to spend more time with her. Maybe I should suggest they even make plans without Aaron. Won't that be fun, and I'm sure Aaron would be very nervous if the Posse joined his mom and his girlfriend for an afternoon of secret sharing while sipping wine. I'll have to get on that right away!

҈

Jenny died. Susan got the call yesterday. People with lung cancer usually suffer a long, slow and painful death. As bad as it is for their family, it has to be worse for the patient. It's hard to imagine anything worse than the pain in Todd's eyes as his mother withered away.

Protective Services took Todd away and put him in temporary foster care. Susan was inconsolable. "That boy just lost the only person in the world who loved him.

He shouldn't be with strangers. He should be here, with us." Susan was wrong. Todd didn't lose the only person who loved him. He still has Susan. She may not see it, but she loves him. We need to find out where he was taken.

Susan went over to Alliance House to go through Jenny's belongings hoping to find someone, anyone who could take Todd so he wouldn't be forced into the system. Distraught and exhausted, she didn't believe it when she first read the letter she found. Jenny wrote a Will about a week ago. She had it witnessed by her doctor and the night nurse. Susan wondered if it was even legal. The Will was short, and direct. The one page document left no questions about Jenny's intentions.

> To Whom It May Concern:
> In life, I didn't have much. My situation always forced me to have the means for a quick escape. I never cared about earthly possessions. The one thing I do cherish is my son, Todd. He is everything to me and I need to be sure he doesn't suffer any more. Here is his birth certificate. His father isn't from around here so don't go looking for him. I want Susan to raise him. She is the only person who ever treated me like I matter. She didn't look at me like I was pathetic or like I was a bad mother. She gave me hope and I want her to give Todd hope. All I ask is that she help him remember me and that he was my reason for living.

Susan left Alliance House frantic. Where was Todd taken and how can she get him back? Jenny didn't want him in foster care, she wanted him with Susan, and Susan was ready to grant the woman her dying wish. But was she ready to raise a little boy?

❧

Aimee decided there is no way she can run her own Nutrition Workshops outside the hospital while still employed there. That doesn't mean she can't start thinking about "life after" the hospital. She is self-certified with five major health insurance companies in the area. This certification allows her to take on clients and be reimbursed by the insurance companies. If she could charge something reasonable, then maybe people would be able to afford the amount insurance won't cover for her classes. She really wants to offer an affordable solution.

Aimee looked at me thoughtfully and asked "Jules, how do you feel about putting that MBA to work? I have an idea and need your help. Could we work out a business plan to offer Nutrition Workshops? I think with a small investment, I could offer an affordable solution that insurance companies would support once they saw the results." What a great idea! Aimee has a wide array of experience including the business savvy of running her own successful businesses. She has worked as a personal trainer for a couple years and a dietician for just as long. She certainly has the experience to make a venture like this successful. All she needs is a business plan with enough potential to impress investors. She wouldn't even need that much money. If you think about it, Weight Watchers often rents space from Churches or Town buildings. It doesn't take much.

I am very excited about the chance. I've written a couple business plans before, but they were for people without the drive to push them forward. I don't even know if my work on those plans was any good because they were never presented. It felt like a lot of work for nothing, but I'm reconsidering that. Maybe I did all that work so when it came time to build a business plan for a business I had an emotional interest in, it wouldn't be my first time.

We have so much to discuss. The first thing I want to put in place is a time line. That often scares people but it won't scare Aimee. She loves deadlines and always does her best to achieve them. Her first one will be a date for a date. When would you like to be captain of your own ship? When would you like to hire the band to play "Take this Job and Shove It"?

Court is in session and Regina is tapping her foot. She can't wait to be done for the day. Aaron asked if she could join him and Sarah for dinner in the North End. Regina didn't care where they were having dinner. You can't get a bad meal anywhere in the North End. As long as they could walk over to Modern Pastry after dinner for coffee and dessert, the night would be perfect in Regina's book. Nothing ended a day quite like a slice of ricotta pie. Regina would go to bed a happy woman with a slice of pie in her belly and another one in the refrigerator for the next night.

Regina told us all about "Judge Judy". I don't remember her real name, I only remember the stories Regina told about her posturing on the bench and speaking as though she was talking into the camera. We dubbed her Judge

Judy after the courtroom drama on TV and the name stuck. Judge Judy loves to hear herself talk. Worse than her droning on, she never seems to have anywhere to be at 4:00. She would often talk on and on until nearly 4:30. At the shuffling of feet, she would look at the clock, strike her gavel and walk out, without as much as a "court dismissed" or even a "good night".

Regina was the one with the shuffling feet today and it was not even 4:00 yet. This day wouldn't end soon enough for her.

At last, and long past 4:00, Regina was free of the court room. She took a deep breath of fresh air on the court house steps and held her face up to the warm sunshine for a minute. After opening her eyes, and stepping into the throng of people leaving work to head home, she set off for the North End. The walk was just over a mile and Regina looked forward to the chance to stretch her legs and clear her head.

Aaron and Sarah were waiting for Regina when she arrived. They all sat at a small table in the corner and chatted animatedly about their days while looking over the menu. When Sarah passed Regina the breadbasket, Regina noticed it – an engagement ring! "Oh my God! You are engaged! When? How? Oh my God! Congratulations!" Regina jumped up to kiss them both then settled back into her chair to hear the whole story.

Aaron began "Yes Mom, Sarah and I are getting married. Remember when I told you she was the one?" Regina did remember. She was pleased to see that he meant it this time. She likes Sarah and thinks they will be good for one another.

"After we met, it took Aaron well over a month to get up the nerve to ask me out. Our first date was last Fourth of July, but it could have been Flag Day" Sarah chided. That was the summer Aaron started working after Grad School. "This year, on Fourth of July, Aaron got a small bottle of champagne to drink while we watched the fireworks. He thought the bubbly would be a nice addition to the excitement and romance of the pyrotechnics."

"I love your story telling Sarah, but please get to it! The suspense is killing me!" Regina exclaimed, only slightly exaggerating.

"Okay, Regina, or should I say Mom, I'll get to it. As he poured the last of the champagne, I saw something sparking in the bottom of my glass. The glittering of the diamond combined with the sparkling of the champagne and crystal flute was nearly blinding."

"Actually, it was her tears that were blinding" Aaron quipped.

Regina heard none of it. Sarah had called her Mom. 'I finally have a daughter', Regina thought. Regina loved Aaron so much she thought her heart would break into pieces from the force of it. Now she'll get to add to it the love of a mother for a daughter. Just wait until the Posse hears we have a wedding to plan!

It's turned cold again. Frankie and I are sitting in front of the fire, our toes stretched out to gather the warmth from the flames. "How are the girls?" he asks? He seldom asks because he's usually circling around us, keeping an eye on things.

"This has been a crazy year. You'd think as we got older, we'd slow our pace a bit and begin to wind down. I don't see that happening for any of us. Lauren is nearing fifty, and she's the baby of the Posse. I am thinking that sixty doesn't sound as old as it used to. It amazes me every day that we aren't in our thirties anymore. Seriously, our kids are all in their thirties. How did this happen?" Frankie knows when I get like this that I just need him to listen. I'm exhausted with everything going on around me, and sometimes, just sometimes, I feel my age. Today is one of them.

Frankie listens patiently for me to get through the complaining. After all these years, he still enjoys hearing about the comings and goings of the Posse. Between Susan's concerns with Todd, Regina on the Grand Jury, Lauren traveling the world and Aimee starting her own business, I talked for the next several hours. I love talking to Frankie about the Posse. He is so compassionate and can see solutions that I'm too close to see. Not only that, but he's thrilled any time one of his suggestions is taken. Tonight's suggestion that I love is that he'd like to spend more time with Todd. The only father figure in his life right now is Susan's dad, and although he's a wonderful guy, he doesn't do much more than sit and talk with him. Frankie can take him out to do "guy stuff". When I realized the added bonus is Susan being freed up for "girl stuff", I love the idea even more. I'll give her a call first thing tomorrow.

Chapter 4
Life as You Knew It

As I expected, Susan was going a bit frantic preparing to bring Todd to his new home. In all the years she and Jenny have been acquaintances at Alliance House, Susan has never had them over to her house. She has always been such a private person, but all that is about to change. She had never been responsible for a child for longer than a weekend and she always had us for backup. That part hasn't changed, we're still here but we are a lot older than we were when our kids were that age.

We went to the Daily Paper for breakfast the next morning. After silently sipping her coffee for what seemed like hours, Susan finally started talking. "How did you do it? One minute you are a single entity, responsible only for yourself and the next minute you are a mother. You no longer come first. Every single minute of your day is focused around your child. Did he sleep well? Did he eat enough? Is he doing okay in school? Is he being bullied? Or bullying?"

Most of us sighed remembering our first days as mothers. It was a long time ago, but some memories stay fresh a long time.

"We all had nine months to get used to the idea of becoming a mother. As daunting is it seems, our babies came needing only to be fed and changed. Sure, it was scary, but it was simpler" I said, truly believing it. I don't know how you take a child with a past distinctly their own and raise them as you see fit. Susan doesn't understand the full history of what Todd lived through before. Even though they have a bond through Jenny and Alliance House, and it won't be like complete strangers becoming family, I'm sure it will be almost as hard.

Lauren has the youngest kids amongst the rest of us. She remembers only too well, "ten wasn't that long ago for the twins. I remember it well. This is when the struggle for independence starts. You'll find he's too old for play dates but too young to hang out at the mall or the movies without an adult."

Susan was worried about getting Todd settled into the right class at school. "I need to register Todd for school on Monday. I have his records but not much else. I hope going to a new school isn't too hard on him. He's been through so much already." School doesn't start for another few weeks, so Todd and Susan can settle in together before any other big changes hit.

"Has he settled in to his room? How did that go?" Aimee liked to keep things orderly and always felt better with everything was in its place. She considered getting Todd settled into his bedroom, getting his backpack set for school and learning the bus route to be a balm to ease the pain of loss the little boy was suffering. Aimee's mom must have muttered the saying "idle hands make devil's work" so often that she can't stop until everything is settled.

Susan was happy relaying the details of their shopping spree. They bought a bed, dresser and desk. They decided to go with a sports motif for the bedding. Susan converted one of the guest rooms into a perfect room for a 'tween'. As we oohhed and ahhed over Susan's retelling of the events, each of us remembered similar rooms in our houses, long since emptied. We pictured the room as spotless, another point of nostalgia for us. No need to point out to Susan that she should remember how sweet and clean the room is now. Once a little boy lives there, it will never be the same again.

Todd will be moving home Sunday afternoon. Susan will call if and when she needs reinforcements. As always, any one of us is just a phone call away!

ಹ∞

As the dog days of summer wore on, Lauren knew they needed to make some serious decisions. It was all so overwhelming. Maybe if they made their decisions independently for each member of the family, it would be easier. There was no reason all the decisions had to be interdependent.

Start with the easy decisions. Carter is going away for college. He wants to live on campus, not at home. He loves his family and where he grew up, but he wants some independence. He needs to get out of Russell's shadow. They are so close, as you'd expect with twins. He wants to learn to rely on himself and not on his twin. He needs the chance to make his own way, his own mistakes, his own friends. Friends that aren't more interested Russell's Olympic prospects than in him. Carter will leave in two weeks to go to Yale University. He met his dorm mate at orientation and they got along well. He'll do just fine. One down.

Shamus is taking the job in Germany. It's a professional stepping stone for better work and a personal reward in recognition of all Shamus has done for the company. General Manager responsible for building a new headquarters is beyond his experience, but Shamus knows this company and its products better than anyone. Shamus' familiarity with the business management will make him successful. He knows it will be hard to be away from the family for so long, but they will all survive. He'll be able to come back for a week every two months. Lauren and the kids will plan extra visits to Shamus in between. Lauren is very supportive of this decision. He wouldn't go if she weren't. The twins are also self-sufficient and with technology, they can talk every day. That's makes two.

If Russell was ever going to compete in the Olympics, 2014 is the year. To qualify, he has to spend this winter competing full time. He has two merchandise manufacturers wooing him for sponsorship. Lauren and I got into a long discussion about the pros and cons of him trying.

"Does Russell have enough passion for the half pipe to drive him to succeed in the daily grind required to make it to the Olympics? Listen to me, like I have any idea what that would entail."

Lauren laughed, "He could be out there all day mastering his tricks regardless of the weather, hunger, daylight but if I ask him to take out the garbage and all I get is flack."

That doesn't surprise me at all. I've seen the girls that gather to watch Russell when he's out there. What young man wouldn't be interested in all that female attention? "I'd be thrilled to be able to point to him on TV and say 'that's our boy!' if he made the team. But Lauren, it will be hard on the family as well. Are you prepared for the travel, stress and the schedule that will be demanded? Of course, that assumes you'll be going on the road with him."

"We haven't decided yet if I'll be going with him. There are coaches and adult chaperones that travel with the team. Some of the competitors are under 18 and they have to have a parent with them. That's not the case with Russell, he's an adult. I don't have to travel with him. I want to, but I also want to be with Shamus in Germany. I don't know if Russell would want me there. He might do better if I'm not there. Less stress I guess."

I could see that. I could also see that Lauren has already decided that she wants Russell to try to make the team. Her pride is overflowing when she talks about his skill, and just qualifying to compete would be gigantic! Even though Lauren didn't voice it, number three is decided.

That leaves one, Lauren and her sabbatical. I wonder when she'll realize taking a year off is what she wants. Soon enough I'm sure. The tough decision for her will be what she does with herself for a year – spend it in Germany with Shamus or travel the competition circuit with Russell. What an absolutely glorious decision to have to make!

ം⊱

It's been over a year since I stopped working and I've never been happier in my life! I can't really say I 'stopped working' since I'm working harder now than I ever did. What I'm doing now is making a difference, a real difference to individuals who I can look in the eye and see that I'm helping. What a wonderful feeling at the end of the day. When I look at the diminishing amount in my bank account, I have to remember the grateful faces of the women I've helped. Women who have been victimized by the people they trusted and then thrust into a system without enough support to help them break free from the cycle.

My work with Alliance House has become well known around the state. I've trained other volunteers who went back and implemented similar programs at other shelters. I need to figure out how to market this concept. I don't want to do it for the money. I want to do it to help others.

As director of Alliance House, Susan goes to many strategizing meetings with directors of shelters across the country. Maybe I should talk to her about promoting the program. If they were willing to send people here for training, think of how many shelters could begin breaking the cycle for the women they help. It would be so much more effective than me going to each shelter.

I need to assess my life. Is this really what I want to do? I traded in a lucrative high tech job for what? To volunteer as a profession coach to abused women. Certainly not a position I aspired to.

A program like this can create significant changes not only the lives of the women we help, but also in their children's lives. If I launch this, and it gains momentum, I can't abandon it. Not that I have a tendency to abandon projects, but this isn't corporate America. I won't have the prestige of a high ranking management title to feed my ego. I've always said that doesn't matter to me, but this would be the proof. I would be formally and officially stepping out of the business arena.

I like the sound of that.

❧

I got a call from Aimee earlier today and she sounded distraught. She wants to get together tonight somewhere quiet where we can talk. We decided to go to the coffee shop across town. It's not Dunkin' Donuts, but they have a nice set up for quiet conversation without a lot of interruption. We decide to meet at 8:00.

"Aimee, you sounded frantic on your voicemail. What's wrong?"

"A client of mine died today."

"What? How could that happen? You are a dietician. You council people how to lose weight. Did a client starve to death?"

"No, the exact opposite. A client came to me for pre-surgery counseling. Through the hospital, the program costs $800 and insurance won't cover it. This woman needed to have open heart surgery but she was too big to have the surgery. She needed to lose 100 pounds before a surgeon would operate. The risks were just too high. So they sent her to our program. When her insurance company refused to pay, she had to drop out."

"Is this the woman you tried to get the hospital to allow in without paying?"

"Yes, but they refused. When I offered to pay for her, they said they would terminate my contract with them and report me to the board. I would have lost my license."

"So what happened?" It was sad this poor women was dead. I was horrified that Aimee was blaming herself. She isn't to blame. If anyone is to blame, it's the hospital for refusing to come up with a work around when the insurance company wouldn't pay.

"When she wasn't allowed into the program, she decided to try to lose weight on her own. She practically starved herself, and then while out walking, she overworked herself and suffered a heart attack. By the time an ambulance got there, she was gone. It isn't fair. She wanted to help herself but she wasn't given the tools. Why did she have to do this on her own? We have the means to help people but we won't do it unless we get the money up front. It's shameful and I hate being part of it."

Aimee had been so happy since she left high tech and became a dietician. She was elated with the successes of clients and felt heart sick for the setbacks. This was beyond anything she had experienced before.

"Aimee, it's possible her heart was so stressed that even with a healthy change of eating and exercise she could have still had a fatal heart attack."

"I know that. If we were working with her on a program and she died of a heart attack, I would be feeling like we tried but were too late. Instead I feel like we didn't try at all. It sucks. It's the one part of the job I hate. I wish there was some way I could offer this program for free. Especially for people who are really trying to make a difference in their lives."

She decides she's all talked out. Maybe she'll feel better in the morning. She has tomorrow off so she's going to spend it in the kitchen testing new recipes. I convince her to invite the Posse over to taste test for her.

☙❧

Some people make their resolutions at the New Year, others do it at their birthdays. For the Posse, we take stock of where we are when the time is right. Tonight feels right.

Susan is new at parenting, and summer ending brings on fresh anxiety for school to begin. In this case, both mother and child were suffering. "Summer's coming to an end. I have Todd's new clothes, backpack, and sneakers. Do you have any idea how fast a ten year old boy's feet grow?" We all laugh. Of course we do. What Susan doesn't know is that a fourteen year old boy's feet grow even faster, and their sneakers cost four times as much! We won't tell her now, but we toast her "To Susan and her excellent job mothering. Being mother hen to all of us has finally paid off! Cheers!"

Lauren is feeling nostalgic tonight as well because she just settled Carter in at college. They drove down alone because Shamus is in Germany and couldn't get home. It was a wistful and tearful goodbye, but they are both handling it okay. Lauren is finishing up at work before her sabbatical starts. She has one week left. "Ever since the twins were born, I constantly considered quitting my job to stay at home with them. Isn't it ironic that now that they are both leaving home, I am finally taking a year off?" It's true. For eighteen years, at every lay off, at every birthday, every illness and broken bone, Lauren considering whether this event should force her hand into quitting. The twins are thriving young adults, thanks to the effort both Lauren and Shamus put in to parenting them. Lauren and Shamus should be incredibly proud of the job they did. I wonder how having Lauren home full time might have changed who the twins grew up to be. Could they be any better kids than they are? Could having her home have backfired? I guess we'll never know.

Regina asks "Lauren, did you decide if you'll be traveling with Russell or spending your time in Germany?" She is such a romantic that she couldn't imagine Lauren and Shamus being separated for a year.

"Yes, I decided I will travel with Russell. I think it's important for him to know I share his dream and will do whatever I can to help him be successful. I want to be sure he is eating right and sleeping enough. He isn't as mature as Carter and I worry about him getting caught up in the party of it all. This way, he and I will share a hotel room on the road, so I know he won't be partying too much." I think that's a wise idea. Russell is a great kid, but even smart, levelheaded kids can be swept away with all that publicity and hype. Hopefully Lauren won't be.

We already talked about Aaron and Sarah's wedding. They haven't set a date yet, but they did decide there will be a special table for the Posse! Marie started that tradition when she got married. My mom sat with my brothers and sisters, while I got to sit with the Posse. It's only right since we shared so much of the child rearing between us. We are looking forward to shopping for dresses together. Once Regina picks out her dress, we'll all get something complementary. We won't look like brides maids, but we'll look as hot as five mature women can look! Men beware!

Regina is a bit stressed that they still haven't decided on a date. "I really want this wedding planned so we can move on to grandchildren. I want to hold a grandbaby of my own and now that Aaron is getting married, I can start dreaming of a grandchild sitting on my lap."

Susan is always annoyed when people push newlyweds to have children right away. "Give him time, Regina! They aren't even married yet. Let them settle in first."

"Settle in? They are both turning 30 soon. Even I can hear their biological clocks ticking." We all laugh and raise our glasses to that.

I'm the only one who noticed that Aimee is being quiet tonight. This is how she recharges. She silently absorbs the energy and love we share. When I reach out to rub her back, she looks up and smiles at me. She knows I'll keep the conversation going and avoid making her share her pain tonight. She will share it with the Posse, just not tonight. Not while it is so raw.

After dessert we clean up and start our goodbyes. Leaving always brings a big commotion followed by a deafening silence. I hope that silence isn't too hard for Aimee to bear tonight. I'll be sure to check up on her tomorrow.

⁓⋄⁓

It was Thursday night, nearly Halloween already. We are all at Susan's having dinner. Todd was debating what to be for Halloween with us. "This is a huge decision m… Susan. I can't be something 'cute'. I don't want the kids to think I'm a baby!" Todd has been struggling with adjusting to Jenny being gone. How does a ten year old come to terms with why his mother had to die? Susan and he are building a strong bond but Todd acts like he's being disloyal to his mother every time they get too close.

Susan has instituted Thursday Night dinners with the Posse. This way, we get one night a week where we can observe their relationship and give her pointers later. She is trying so hard, maybe too hard, to get it right. The uncomfortable moments tonight were glaringly obvious. What should they call each other?

After Todd heads to bed, we sit back and relax. I begin "you are doing such a wonderful job becoming a mother to Todd. He is flourishing under your love and guidance. You should be so proud of what you've accomplished."

Susan isn't buying it. "There is still something between us. He isn't connected to me like other boys with their mom's. I know in the coming years he'll pull away, but if he starts this far away already, I'm afraid I'll lose him completely."

Lauren jumps in, "I remember with the twins. Carter and I started fighting like cats and dogs when he was ten. Or was it nine? It felt like he was so young when it started. He got along fine with Shamus. Russell on the other hand treats both of us like we are just two groupies, like all the others. Some days I feel like he couldn't pick me out of a line up." We all know Lauren doesn't believe that, but she was so close to Russell as a little guy. When he started skate boarding, he started emotionally breaking away. I think this next year will be great for the two of them. I believe the old saying whatever doesn't kill you makes you stronger.

"Susan, I think you should have a conversation with Todd about what you should call each other." The girls look at me with questions all over their faces. "Titles are so important and build that bond of belonging. You need that with Todd. Remember when you were growing up and your friends all called your parents mister and misses So-And-Such? Then remember when you grew up and you introduced adult friends or even your husband to your parents? It was always so awkward. What do they call them? For years Frankie never called my parents anything. When we talked about them, he would call them 'your mother or your father'. Well, Todd is in that same boat and so are you." Sometimes I get on my soap box and can't find a way to step off it.

Susan retorted "It isn't that simple. It doesn't matter what we call each other."

Aimee was slowly agreeing with me. "Susan, when you take him into school, what do you say for introductions?"

"Simple, 'Hi, I'm Susan and I'm bringing Todd into school.' No titles required."

I won't give up. "Do you think that makes him feel like he belongs to you? Forever? It doesn't sound like it to me. Don't you think 'Hi, I'm Susan, and this is my son Todd' sounds much more permanent?"

"Yes", Susan agrees, "but what if he doesn't want me to call him my son? That will break my heart."

At long last we all agree having a discussion about it is the best idea. If they aren't comfortable with Mom and son, they can come up with alternatives. Susan decides they will talk about it over the weekend. They'll go out for breakfast and talk before going to the Halloween outlet to get a really gross and not at all cute Halloween costume suitable for a big guy, not a baby.

Susan certainly has her hands full!

Since I'm still not working a "real" job, I decide to meet Regina for breakfast before she heads to work. As usual, she walks the mile from the train to the diner. "The temperature in Boston is starting to drop and next week we turn the clocks back" Regina reported glumly. She is such a sun worshiper and hates to see the days growing shorter and temperatures dropping.

Regardless, she refuses to give up her morning or afternoon walks to and from the train. "Doesn't that wind rip right through you when you walk between those buildings downtown?"

"Sure, but if you dress right and avoid going out with wet hair…" she trails off. It's always been a sticking point between Regina's mother and me that I always leave the house in the morning with wet hair.

"Not you too! You have become your mother!" We both laugh at that.

"Are you working on any interesting cases?" I'm always surprised that people can be so conniving and cruel to one another. I'd be terrible on the grand jury because I'd want to talk to the guilty people and say 'what were you thinking? What you did wasn't nice.' Somehow I imagine they already know that.

Rather than disclose any case details, Regina distracts me with the scenery she's been observing in the courthouse. "A suit and tie can make any man look respectable, professional and trustworthy. Half the time I spot an attractive man and think he must be a lawyer but he turns out to be a defendant."

"Not all the accused are guilty" I quickly retort.

"Maybe that's true, but I think I stand a better chance of meeting a man without a record outside the courthouse."

"Sure", I agree, "By the way how much longer are you on this jury anyway?"

"I should be done the end of December. I think they go on break the week before Christmas, and that should be it for me. I will go back to work the first week of January."

I can't imagine being gone from work for six months. How do you pick back up like you were never gone? Think of everything that could have changed in that time. At my old company, we could have been bought , sold, or had a lay off or two. I don't miss those days at all!

ॐॐ

Lauren and Russell are leaving for his first competition. They are heading to Colorado. I still haven't figured out why the half pipe competitions have to be near a ski resort. They only require cold, not mountains. I guess if they need to make snow, it's easier to be near a resort.

Lauren shows us her schedule. Russell will be competing or traveling every day for the next four months. That is crazy! He needs to place in the top six at ninety percent of the events to make the team. If he places between 6th and 10th, he'll be an alternate. It's going to be rigorous but they'll handle it.

We put together a web site for both of them to post pictures, videos and blogs. It will be a nice way for Lauren to update everyone at once. Then when we do connect on the phone, we can talk about more interesting things.

We all want to know how she and Russell are surviving living in such tight quarters. More importantly, we want to know how she and Shamus are doing being apart. Lauren will sneak away half way through to visit Shamus for a few days. Shamus and Carter will both join Lauren and Russell over Christmas. Let me remember, they will be spending Christmas in Southern France. Yes, they'll be skiing the Alps as one big happy family.

Sipping her morning tea, Aimee glances at the winning numbers for the lottery. No way, it can't be! We won! Aimee has been playing the same number for the Posse for twenty years. We always talked about splitting the winnings, retiring and never looking back! After all those years, we hit! Aimee quickly calls us all together to give us the good news! In all our years of playing, we never expected a celebration like this!

Susan has always been the financial planner amongst us. Thank God for her! Aimee and I are as far away from Susan on the financially responsible scale as you can get. If it weren't for Susan, we would still be living paycheck to paycheck without a nest egg to fall back on. Maybe not that bad, but close. We all decide to see what Susan thinks we should do with the money. I'm thinking a cruise around the world would be fun, but since I'm the only one not working, I'm the only one with enough time on my hands for that. Unfortunately the money isn't enough for us all to retire right now. What to do, what to do…

We decide to divide the money equally and invest however we want. Most of us put our money into a retirement account. There is hope of retiring now, someday before we're dead. We also decide not to mention the windfall to anyone outside the Posse. No need to have all our relatives coming out of the woodwork looking to borrow money we'll never get back. Nope, let's keep it quiet, and if we want to, there's nothing stopping us from spreading it a bit whenever the need arises or the fancy is tickled.

As the holidays approach, I decide I'm really not in the mood for a big celebration. The kids will be busy with their own families and making them split the holidays between us and their in-laws is such a stress. Frankie and I talk about it and decide to make it simpler for everyone and go away for the couple weeks surrounding Christmas.

"Are you sure you can give up seeing the faces of the grandkids opening their presents on Christmas morning? You always want to be at both Marie's and Jason's houses for the commotion", Frankie asked me over coffee this morning. He knows better than anyone how much the holiday means to me. He tried to rein me in for many years when my lavish ideas got out of hand and I went crazy in the toys stores. I was the same when our kids were little. The last few years were different. Maybe it is because we have everything we could ever want. Maybe it's because those grandbabies of ours have nearly a toy store full of things themselves. Whatever the reason, I have not been buying toys all year long. Instead, I've come up with ideas for each of the children and grandchildren that involve spending quality time together and not another object to get tossed in a closet. Marie and I will be spending a long weekend at a Spa. There is one in Connecticut that I've been to with the Posse that I know Marie will love. Frankie and Jason will be going to Florida to take in the races at the Daytona 500. Then we'll be taking both families on a cruise to Alaska in the summer.

I can't imagine any way this won't be a better gift than another X-box game or Barbie accessory. How many town houses can one girl have? "Yes Frankie, I am thrilled with the gift ideas this year! I can't wait to tell them. My only alteration is that I think we should invite Adam to join you and Jason and Rebecca to join Marie and I. I really think they would appreciate being included. What do you think?" We have always treated our son- and daughter-in-law as though they are our own blood. By all rights, they should be included in this.

"I agree that is the right thing to do, but Jason and Adam are pretty close and I'm afraid I'll be left out. I guess I can try to avoid that. Besides, they are the ones that need to stick together in the long run. Once we retire and I take you away" and he trailed off. We always dreamed of retiring somewhere romantic. Wouldn't that be great if it could come true? "I know we can't leave for good quite yet, but I have a surprise for you." He handed me an envelope.

I love surprises! I take the envelope and rip it open. Airline tickets to... Key West! "We're going to Key West? When? " I ask. I love Key West. The last time I was there was a long time ago with the Posse. We ended up getting stranded there while Massachusetts was buried in a blizzard. There was over three feet of snow here and the power was out for more than four days in many parts. Schools and businesses were closed. The whole time, we were "stuck" in Key West, sipping margaritas and soaking up the rays. We had to extend our trip by three days since the return flights were backed up. For some reason, no one felt sorry for us. I never understood that.

"We leave the day after we celebrate Christmas with the kids and don't come back for two weeks."

Wow, two weeks in paradise. Unless we get a blizzard back here and the trip is extended again. A girl can pray!

∂∞∂

The next time we are together, Susan is so much more relaxed and as expected, we bombard her with questions. "What's up, Susan? How come you are so relaxed? Is motherhood finally agreeing with you?"

"Todd and I had a long conversation about our relationship, stability and the future. He thought I didn't want him to call me mom because I didn't want to keep him. I'm not surprised. I heard stepchildren often feel less loved by the 'new' parent. In Todd's case, he doesn't have any 'real' parents to fall back on. He felt totally unwanted."

That poor boy had been through so much. He must have such a hard time trusting that Susan will always be there. I can see why this is so important. It's really the foundation they'll be building on.

"We decided I will call him 'my son'. That way, there is no question that he belongs to me. Todd's going to call me 'my Susan'. This allows him to stake ownership of me without dismissing the memory of his mother. That wound is so fresh we can't tread there right now. We both decided this works for now. We might change it later, but for now we won't be stumbling over titles anymore making introductions uncomfortable."

I really like that solution. Belonging is so important. Now they both have someone they can claim as their own and are needed by someone. It's a magical combination. Susan is so lucky to have the opportunity to help Todd grow into a responsible, conscientious adult. I'm thrilled that Todd has the opportunity to help Susan realize her life can't revolve around just work anymore. When you give love, it comes back multiplied. I can't wait for Susan and Todd to reap the bounty of that lesson!

Chapter 5
In Walks a Stranger

Regina will finish up on the Grand Jury the Friday before Christmas. We decide to celebrate early so it doesn't get lost in the holiday fray. No matter how small or grand, the Posse always takes the time to celebrate our achievements. This one will be a pot luck dinner at my house.

Regina is looking at the end of her tenure on the Grand Jury with melancholy. "I won't miss hearing all the gore and corruption from the cases every day, but I'm not excited about going back to work", she said. "Things have changed in the six months she was away from the office. It's going to be like starting a new job."

I ask how she's celebrating her last day working in Government Center.

"I'm going to take myself to a Bruins game. They are in town Friday night and should have at least one ticket available for sale." Regina has always loved the Bruins and watched them at every opportunity. When Aaron was little, she'd drag him to games. Once he made it known he didn't like the games, she started going alone. Regina has never had any trepidation doing things on her own. Whether it's going out for a nice dinner, to the movies, or to a game, if she wants to do it and no one wants to join her, she'll go alone. I'm so proud of her for that.

"They're playing Montreal and those games are always great. I'll grab a bite to eat first then head to the game." Little does she know what's in store for her that night...

☙❦

Lauren and Russell have been on the road for over two months. The rest of the Posse went to visit Carter to spoil him a bit. We were afraid he'd get lonesome without any of his family around. We took him and a few friends out for dinner. After the boys consumed more food than I ever thought possible, we took Carter grocery shopping. We wanted to be sure he had plenty of everything especially since his mom wasn't around to make a special delivery.

While we were out, we got an update from Lauren. Russell had competed in his first qualifying event and placed 4th overall! He had an amazing showing and Lauren captured some great photos and video to go up on the blog. We are all so proud of Russell and wish we could all be there. Shamus has been adding to the blog as well. It started out with him adding comments to Lauren and Russell's entries but lately, he's been posting his own progress. I told Carter that he should start posting there as well. It could become a family memoir of the year they scattered.

I talked to Lauren yesterday. She's having a blast, but is a bit itchy for something to do. Shortly after we start talking, Lauren finds herself whining "every day, I get up and head down to the practice area. I stand around stomping my feet all day trying to stay warm. I wish there was something I could do to be useful."

I quickly fall in to solution mode and offer an idea, "did you ask the coach if there's anything you could do? Could you time them or take photos? Maybe you could take videos to give each competitor so they can study their performance and correct mistakes. Or would that be potentially helping Russell's competition?"

"That's a great idea. I'll ask. Russell's coach is working with two other contenders. Maybe I could work with the three of them. That would be a good start. I'll get some awesome video of Russell then post it to the blog and have him look at it. Thanks for the idea. I think my brain is frozen, which is why I couldn't think of anything."

క∞

Aimee is falling into a funk. She is depressed about the inability to offer the weight loss classes to people who can't afford the steep price the hospital insists on. She's tried to get it approved by the insurance companies, she's tried to get the hospital to lower the price or offer scholarships. No one is willing to make it easier for people to afford.

I came up with an alternative, "What do you think it would cost to sponsor the program? Let's try to figure it out. Maybe if we took the lottery money, we could put it in a trust and apply the interest to run the program."

Aimee really had no idea how much it would cost to run the program. "If we could figure out the cost to run the program, we could go solicit funding from... I don't know where you get funding for medical programs? If that fails, I could figure out how long my share of the lottery winnings would last. I can't take the winnings from the rest of the Posse."

There's a big difference between us offering her money and Aimee taking it. I need to talk to the others.

"Aimee, can you figure out how much money it would take to run your program for a year? Put in all the bells and whistles with a breakdown of the costs. We could put together a business plan and solicit investors. Based on the amount invested, Aimee could tailor her offering to be something she could sustain. This is very exciting! If we can't get initial investors, the Posse could invest. Once the program becomes self-sustaining, Aimee could return our money. Sure, it's a risk, but what isn't? Personally, I'd rather invest my money on Aimee. Based on the return I've been getting on my 401K, I can't imagine Aimee doing any worse!

On Regina's last day at the courthouse, she left with a plan. At 4:00, she took her leave and went to Al Dente's for a lovely dinner of chicken saltimbocca and four-cheese risotto. Yum! After dinner she strolled slowly toward the Boston Garden. The Bruins were playing the Canadians and the game didn't start until just after 8:00. She had plenty of time. Since Regina discovered that it was easy to get a single ticket, she treated herself to a couple games a season. She was always lucky enough to sit near friendly people who included her in their game time banter and she'd come home exhilarated from the excitement, whether her Bruins actually won or lost.

Regina went up to the ticket booth and requested a single ticket. "I'm sorry, we're sold out." Regina was taken back. "You're kidding? I can always get a single ticket." Apparently there was a big college event and they bought up all the remaining tickets.

"Excuse me, are you looking for a ticket?" Regina turned around to see a man around her age holding a single ticket. She had always considered scalping tickets illegal, for both the person selling the ticket as well as for the person buying it. If this guy was asking right in front of the ticket booth, could it really be a criminal act?

"Is this legal?" Regina asked the ticket agent. The agent looked at the ticket and assured Regina that the ticket was authentic and one of a season ticket. The man selling it claimed that he typically brought his son to games with him. His son recently relocated and couldn't make it to Boston for games any more. He'd been scalping the second ticket all season. The ticket agent confirmed he had seen the man there for other games and assured Regina that if she bought the ticket for face value, not more, then no crime would be committed.

Regina turned to the man and asked his price. After the money changed hands, Regina and the stranger walked into the game together. This could be a great game Regina thought as she assessed the man's ringless left hand.

His name is Joe. He grew up in Eastie also and is the same age as one of Regina's older brothers. They didn't know each other because Joe went to Catholic school through high school. Regina's brothers certainly did not! He was married for 17 years and got divorced the year after his son left for college. The similarities to Regina's life were startling. All of that and he loves hockey enough to have season tickets too. Could this get any better?

As they were walking out of the Garden after the game ended, Regina said "If you ever want to get rid of a ticket, give me a call." Joe reminded her that he had a spare ticket for the entire season. He insisted she should call him if she wanted to go to a game, and 'save me from a life of crime scalping my tickets'. They both chuckled over her innocence. Regina liked the camaraderie she felt and decided that she would call him to get another ticket. While she's at it, she'll invite him to join her for a pre-game dinner.

As expected, Regina had to get the Posse together to discuss all the details of meeting Joe. We only had one day before Christmas began in earnest, so we all juggled and shuffled to have a quick dinner with Regina on Saturday. We all showed up at her house for dinner. She cooked her amazing manicotti. We all act like she'd never share her secret family recipe, but it's mainly because we want her to cook it for us.

Susan started in first, "I can't believe you don't remember who won the game!" Regina is a die-hard Bruins fan. This guy certainly distracted her if she couldn't remember the score.

Regina was quick to respond, "I know who won, I did." I am so happy for Regina. She has been looking for love for a long, long time. She is one of the most sincere people I know, generous with her time and her heart. She gives so much of herself to all of us. It's time for her to find a man that deserves her.

"Tell us all about him!" The details Regina gave initially are unusual for most people, but they are the things Regina notices. "He was very polite to the ticket taker and the people helping you find your seats. He knew where his seats were, but he still let people do their job and he showed them appreciation. He let me have my choice of seats, pointing out the pros and cons of each." We had had enough of these details proving he was a nice guy, we wanted some stats! Come on Regina. Finally we got the details, tall, dark, handsome and single. Perfect. Once we'd talked enough about Joe to picture him, but not enough to jinx it, we moved on to other topics.

I can't believe Christmas is essentially over and I didn't wrap a single present! I'm a little bit melancholy as Frankie and I move aside our winter clothes to pack for our trip to the Florida Keys. We leave tomorrow morning for Miami, then rent a car and slowly meander south. Frankie just smiles at me. He's been trying to get me to tone down my December festivities for years.

We had a big celebration with the kids and grandkids yesterday. We were explicit – no presents. We told everyone about our plans to take them on vacations, not as Christmas presents but to spend a little bit of what they would have inherited. We decided to give the kids their choice for the adult vacations. The boys picked the Daytona 500 over Spring Training with Frankie and the girls picked the spa in Connecticut over Las Vegas with me. I'm thrilled. Frankie is a little disappointed. Maybe he and I will go to spring training some year.

Nothing topped the grandkids' excitement when we told them where we were all going in the summer! Two weeks in Alaska, cruising and exploring. They were beside themselves with excitement. I need to be sure when I book the cabins to have the kids near each other and Frankie and I on the opposite end and a different floor.

Okay, enough reliving the holiday celebration with the family. Now it's time to focus on finishing this packing so we can start our vacation. I can almost feel the warm sun caressing my skin. What a minute, I do believe that is Frankie's hand. So much for packing…

༺❦༻

I got a call from Susan shortly after returning from vacation. Her mom is getting worse. She fell and broke her hip and is in rehab. Her dad is spending every day driving back and forth to the rehab center and is wearing himself out.

Susan was quick to praise the positive influence Todd has been on them. "Todd has been a God-send with both my parents. They absolutely glow when he calls them Nana and Papa. Todd loves the attention they lavish on him. He's had so little family over the years, that he soaks up any attention he gets. Todd's chatter helps the day pass for mom. Since she fell, she can't do much anyway. Now dad gets a break when Todd is there."

I ask if there is anything I can do? Anything any of us can do.

"Yes", Susan admits slowly, surprising both of us with the admission, "could you research some assisted living homes for seniors? I think it's time they move into one of those places that are like a condo but have cafeterias with meals and doctors on site. I think I'll be able to convince them after this."

This is a huge step for Susan. I don't mean admitting her parents are aging, but actually asking for help. We are her closest friends but she would never ask us for help before. I guess becoming a mom has taught her that you can't do everything by yourself. It's okay to let someone help every once in a while.

My old neighbor moved into an assisted living place she loves. I'll talk to her and the management there to see if they can recommend a place close to Susan. Now that Susan has Todd, I want to do everything I can to keep Todd and his grandparents stay close.

Lauren had posted pictures from Russell's last competition and we decided to watch those together. He is truly amazing! I think he has a real chance at winning the Olympics, but I'm not much of a judge. Lauren will be away for Easter and we agreed to swoop in and take Carter for a holiday weekend as only the Posse can celebrate. He is looking forward to it. There is a time when kids aren't allowed to hang with us – the years between learning to talk and earning the right to vote in a national election. Our daughters all looked forward to the day they can be included as women. I remember the day Marie was welcomed. She was thrilled. Our weekends away were never much interest to the boys, but we'll make an exception next weekend with Carter. We won't drag him to a spa and instead will take him to New York City for a weekend on the town!

I had some of my own news to share. "After 15 months unemployed and loving every moment of it I must add, I decided I won't be going back to work. Since I've been unemployed, I've gotten such satisfaction from working with the women at Alliance House. I love to see people break out of the cycle of abuse they have been suffering through and gain the confidence to make a better life for themselves and their children. Also, working with Aimee on her business plan for the Wellness Center has been awesome. Obviously, Aimee isn't an abused women, but she was a women stuck in the grind of corporate America. Helping her break free of that brings a similar satisfaction. I have spent my entire career looking for the perfect boss. And I think I've found her. Me."

"Here, here! A toast to working for a boss who appreciates your effort!" Susan shouted as she raised her glass. Regina was speechless. She had pushed me to do this for years, and her pride for me was visible on her face. "To a boss that cares passionately about her clients", Aimee added with heartfelt praise.

We continued our celebration until late into the night. None of us wanted to leave but we knew it was time.

"Skype is a wonderful thing" Lauren is thrilled to be able to see us all as she calls from her PC while waiting in the airport with Russell. We had just dropped Carter at the airport and called to let Lauren know he was on his way.

They are all getting together in Germany to see how Shamus is progressing on the office building. Carter decided to study Civil Engineering in addition to Politics and has the idealistic attitude of someone with a little information and grand ideas. Shamus will have such a good time dazzling him with details of the development site.

Typical of our gatherings, we are all talking at once. Lauren is laughing so hard she's crying. "As much as I love experiencing this with Russell, I miss you guys like crazy! Russell just doesn't understand the fine art of lingering over coffee and dessert and how that can take longer than the entire dinner!" We miss Lauren too, but it is easier for us since we still have each other.

Lauren gave us the run down on Russell's statistics. He has three more competitions before Olympic training begins. If he places in the top ten in two of them, he is on the team. If not, he's an alternate. Either way, Russell was going to the 2014 Olympics! We are all so excited for Russell. Then she tells us she'll be coming home to us in four weeks.

"Have a wonderful time in Germany with the whole family. I hope Carter doesn't decide to drop out of college and take up with a burlesque German barmaid!" Susan said over a laugh.

Lauren retorted "Susan, now that you're a mother, you are going to have to stop joking like that. These things have a way of coming back to bite you."

A few minutes later we ended the call. Hanging up is always bittersweet.

Todd has settled into his new life new family and school. Susan has legally adopted him and they are a happy little family. Todd has even started picking up some of Susan's traits, including her thirst for knowledge and that was challenging her.

"Does anyone remember Algebra?" Susan asked exasperated while sitting down with the Posse for dinner. We all laughed! Lauren was the last of us going through this with the twins. All of us have struggled through junior high and high school homework with our kids. Susan had a long road ahead of her!

"I don't get it", Aimee complained, "we all have college degrees. Why is this so hard? What in the world do parents who didn't go to college do?"

Regina said "I'm convinced that they don't have the layers of useless information on top of their memories of Algebra and are likely a lot more help to their kids." I agree. It had been so long since I'd seen a quadratic equation that I couldn't be of any help. Susan was on her own for this parenting nightmare.

Luckily for Susan, her worries about her parents living on their own are over. Her parents settled into an assisted living center about 10 minutes from her and they love it. They have a two bedroom condo with easy access to all the amenities including an indoor pool and cafeteria. Susan's mom recovered from her broken hip but is still nervous navigating stairs. This place is perfect for them. There are plenty of new people that her dad can entertain with his many stories. Her mom found a group of women who love to play Scrabble as much as she does. There are doctors, hairdressers and shops on premises, so they never have to leave. Susan is able to visit often and Todd's bus drops him there after school. It couldn't have worked out better for them.

Since Jenny died and left Todd to Susan, Susan has reprioritized. She still loves her job and has maintained her high work ethic, but she now balances that with her family. Her son.

Chapter 6
Wedding Bells

"Aaron and Sarah set their wedding date to December 28! They will be getting married in a mansion on the waterfront in downtown Boston." Regina is beside herself! She has always loved winter weddings and can't wait to see what colors Sarah picks for the dresses and flowers. Her eyes glass over with tears of happiness as she tells us all the details.

"You will be the most beautiful Mother of the Groom in history!" I can't wait. Regina has been so excited about gaining a daughter and she and Sarah get along perfectly. I'm sure Sarah will include Regina in the wedding planning.

Regina is proud to report "Aaron wants the Posse to have a special role in their wedding." Aaron had grown up with us interfering in every moment of his life. At times he acted exasperated. Really, who needs five mother hens watching their every move?

"I guess he's forgiven us for embarrassing him at his prom?" Aimee asks. She knows we did the same thing for every one of our kids, but Aaron's date was particularly overwhelmed by the onslaught of cameras and crazy women shouting 'look this way', 'no, over here'.

Regina has already decided she wants to get a dress of Christmas red satin. That decision practically dictates that the rest of the Posse will deck themselves in other jewel toned satins. We just have to wait to be sure Sarah doesn't pick red for the bridesmaids. Hopefully she'll decide soon, because we want to go shopping soon!

෴

It's been years since I got my MBA, but I still have most of my books in the attic. Frankie went up to find them and lugged them down to me. Helping Aimee with her business plan encouraged me and now I want to write my own business plan. I want to have a consulting company to help women of all walks of life gain their independence and step out on their own.

If Aimee and I could both get financial backing for our plans, I could begin a portfolio to attract other entrepreneurial women. I would focus on women seeking bank loans who needed to produce a credible business plan to be presented and invested in. With two successes under my belt, hopefully I could attract more clients. I'd have to figure out how to charge for these services, and that would fund my volunteer work with shelters.

Frankie helped by shooting holes in my proposal and helping me formulate novel ideas for asking for money. We also worked out a detailed budget to determine how much money I would have to make to make this worth my effort. Our house was paid off. Our children were grown and self-sufficient. We were comfortable. I didn't need to make much. I really only needed to break even. I was at a point in my life that I could do something for society. To me, that seemed like a perfect way to spend my last few years before retirement.

My career redirection has given Frankie the motivation to look at his own career. He has been a professor in the Computer Science Department at University of Massachusetts for 20 years and Dean of the Department for the last six years. He is getting ready to slow down himself. Maybe our exit strategy should be considered as a major component to my business plan. Wouldn't it be nice to retire while we are still young enough to enjoy it!

Aimee went to visit her son and his family in Washington DC. She hadn't seen them since Christmas and she was desperate to hug those grandbabies. Michael is a lawyer and though he doesn't have much business experience, Aimee asked him to review her business plan.

Michael thought the plan was sound and could be profitable if she could get insurance companies to back her. He knew people in the business and asked her permission to share the plan with them.

Aimee was quick to agree but explained the business model in more detail. "I don't really need a lot of money invested. If I get the approval of multiple insurance companies, I'll be able to get referrals from doctors."

The next day, Michael invited a couple friends to dinner who also happen to be on the health advocate council for the Insurance Association of America. Dinner discussion proved how passionate Aimee was about her business and she was able to convince everyone that it was a win-win proposal. "If people are able to lose weight, they will have less health problems and therefore be less burden to insurance companies or the government."

Michael' wife insisted on a change of subject before Michael opened the Scotch and she brought out dessert. Everyone was happy to agree, but not before asking Aimee if she could present her ideas to the board personally. Aimee called me after everyone left gleeful! "You'll have to come with me! I get so nervous when presenting and this is so important." It was important to both of us and I was honored Aimee asked!

ଛଚ

Hockey season was winding down and Regina was getting together regularly with Joe for dinner before or after games. They had been to at least half a dozen games together and out to dinner many more times than that. "Don't you think it's time the Posse met Joe?" I asked when Regina got that dreamy look in her face. "You've been dating him for over two months already and no one's met him yet."

"We aren't dating, we are just hanging out together." We both knew she was crazy as she said it, but I tried to keep a straight face. She was reluctant to bring him home because she lived in the same house she shared with her ex-husband all those years ago. She didn't want any ghosts hanging around when they brought their relationship to the next level. Regina wondered if that was the same reason Joe didn't invite her to his place.

This wasn't like Regina at all. "You must really like this guy to be playing it so safe" I said. Regina blushed and looked down at her feet. "Come on Regina, you need to make a move. Why don't you invite him away for a weekend? There you can tell him about your reluctance and show him that a change of scenery is great for both of you!"

A slow smile came over Regina's face. "I can never hide anything from you. You always see right through me. I think that's a great idea. We are having dinner tomorrow night. I'll ask him."

Regina decided a winter weekend at Cape Cod would be fun. It's far enough away that an overnight stay would be easily justifiable, not that either of them had anyone to justify the trip to. Long strolls on a cold beach would be a great prelude to a warm soak in a hot tub and who knows where that would lead? Perfect!

"So, now that that's settled, when will we get to meet him?"

ත⋅ශ

As spring approached, Lauren got ready for Carter to return from school. We warned her that it's never easy getting kids back to obeying house rules after they've been away, and she's a bit nervous. Russell will be home for a few weeks prior to heading to Russia to begin final training. Shamus just completed the German office and hopes to be home for good in about a month. It had been a year since they were all together at home, not on a short vacation somewhere around the world. As much as they wanted to spend the time alone together, Lauren and Shamus realized everyone would want to spend time with Russell and Carter before they left again for another year.

Lauren decided to have parties three weekends in a row. The first would be for the twins friends, kids from school, parents Shamus or Lauren got to know through sports and PTA, and neighbors. The second party was for the twins friends again and coworkers of Lauren and Shamus's. Seems that everyone wanted to wish Russell luck in the competitions and to earn bragging rights that they shook his hand, that same hand that accepted the gold medal! The last party was for family. Some people, like the Posse were invited to all three. It was an array of bittersweet celebrations. Both kids were growing up, and going off a second time on their own. Shamus and Lauren would be home without kids. It would be their first taste of what life will be like when the twins finish college and are on their own. After a year separation, Lauren is certainly looking forward to the undivided attention of her husband!

ಗಿಳ

It's been almost a year since Regina first bought that fateful Bruins ticket from Joe and they began their romance. He is a great guy and she's very happy. We are spending more time together because Frankie and Joe get along so well. We don't have to leave them home and get grief over all the time we spend with the Posse while they sit at home all alone.

We spend a lot of afternoons in Boston, going to a museum for a couple hours then to a pub for an early dinner. We all love to people watch so the fall has been great, sitting in the outdoor cafes watching the crowds stroll by.

"What's their story?" Frankie asks as a couple in their forties walks by, she is casting sideway glances at him while he walks on with purpose. He has always loved playing that game. Over the years, we have become rather elaborate in our explanations, and Regina and Joe are quickly catching on.

"Oh let me take this one", Regina says. "They just got a call from their daughter in college. She was at a party last night and a guy came up to her and claimed he was her brother. She laughed it off at the time. Today when talking to her parents on their weekly call, she mentioned it to her mother. When her father heard, he got angry and said we are going down there. He hasn't said another word since. His wife is scared. She doesn't know what secret she is about to learn about her husband." What an imagination!

"That's great" I say, "but what do people walking by think of us?"

"Again, an easy one" Regina says. "They look at us and think those two couples are the luckiest people alive to be so happily in love." With that, Frankie reaches over to give me a kiss. Not to be outdone, Joe follows suit with Regina. We all crack up laughing when we hear a nearby teenager mutter "get a room".

Christmas came and went in a low-key manner this year. Forgoing gifts for vacations together was such a hit last year, we decided to do it again. This year, I'll be taking Jason and Adam to Las Vegas for a couple of shows, some awesome meals and a bit of gambling. Frankie will take Marie and Rebecca to New York City for some classic New York pizza, a couple Broadway shows and a horse drawn carriage ride through Central Park. The family trip will be to the Grand Canyon. I can't wait to see everyone's face when they get there and find out we'll be watching the sunrise in a hot air balloon over the canyon! None of us have ever been to the Grand Canyon, so it should be a grand trip for sure!

Since I proved I'm capable of keeping Christmas low-key, Frankie trusts me to stay home this year. As much as I loved being whisked off to Key West last year, Frankie decided to trust that I wouldn't sneak out on shopping sprees. We celebrate with a quiet dinner for two in front of a roaring fire. As we reflect on our lives, we admit we wouldn't change a thing. Life has been good to us and those we love. You can't ask for much more than that.

Our kids and grandkids planned a brunch for us overlooking Boston Harbor on Boxing Day. Depending on how this goes, I think we should make it a new tradition. We'll put all the stress of sharing the holiday's with all the parents right out of their celebration. That is a gift in of itself.

Tonight is the rehearsal for Aaron and Sarah's wedding. I can't wait for the festivities to begin!

༄༅

With Christmas over, it's time to get into wedding mode, quickly! The wedding rehearsal went off without a hitch.

Since it was also Boxing Day, the groomsmen couldn't help teasing the bride by showing up for rehearsal in boxing shorts, satin robes and boxing gloves. We all laughed through the insanity of the best man searching for the rings in his shorts wearing boxing gloves.

The night was mild for the end of December and Sarah looked gorgeous on the eve of her wedding. The love on Aaron's face was so obvious that I can't begin to imagine what he'll do when he sees her tomorrow. Aaron will walk each of us in, two at a time, then Regina alone. Then he'll take his place up front. I know this is typically done by an usher, but Aaron didn't want anyone else responsible for the Posse. Regina was crying through the entire rehearsal. She will be a mess tomorrow.

We had a festive dinner in the North End with lots of toasts and laughs as everyone reminisced with stories of Aaron or Sarah growing up. Sarah's family fit in perfectly with everyone, and I think if her mother were local, she could easily join in with our Posse. All too soon it was time to head back to our rooms so we would be fresh for the morning. While we spend the time making ourselves gorgeous, the men would be keeping Aaron from going crazy with nerves.

The big day arrived and a band of hair stylists and makeup artists arrived. The Posse was getting ready together in Regina's room. When we decided this all those months ago, we thought she'd be alone in the room. That was not to be! Joe was sharing this event with Regina and we couldn't be happier. Joe was with Aaron, Frankie, Shamus and the groomsmen right now.

Regina was gorgeous in her ruby red satin dress and her hair pulled back with a bejeweled clip. Her makeup was waterproof and tear proof. Hopefully she'll make it through the day with minimal damage. I was wearing an emerald green dress and make up! Frankie will be amazed to see me. I seldom wear makeup and you'd think with the admiration he gives me every time I do, I would do it more often. It's so much work to look beautiful! Lauren had on a sapphire dress she bought while in Germany with Shamus. She had saved it for a special occasion, and this wedding fit the bill! Aimee picked a brilliant amethyst dress which looked perfect with her blond hair. She didn't care how old her license claimed she was, she would never let her blond hair go gray! Susan wore in a sleek amber dress that proved becoming a mom did not ruin shape! She had always been the only one of us able to pull off those form fitting, narrow skirted dresses and she still can! Regina gave us each the same hair clip she wore. It had dazzling stones that complimented each of our dresses and the unity of us wearing them wouldn't be missed by anyone. The hair stylist artfully arranged our hair around the clip. We looked lovely, if I do say so myself.

When Aaron came to gather us up for the ceremony, he was blown away. "You women are gorgeous! I sure hope Sarah is able to steal the show from you!" We all appreciated the praise but we knew once he saw Sarah, no other women would matter. We all gathered what we needed and headed downstairs. We were grateful Regina and Joe got a room in the same building as the ceremony. We might look great, but we were walking in heels. We try to avoid that as much as possible.

Once we were all seated, Aaron took his place up front. Instead of an altar, there was an elegant fireplace festively decorated for a wedding. When the music began and Sarah walked in, the room went silent. Her gown was white with bits of red peeking out from underneath. Her flowers were long stemmed red roses she carried cradled in her arms. Her attendants were the mirror image, in red gowns with white roses. It was a fairy tale Christmas wedding.

None of us knew Aaron and Sarah had written their own vows. In Aaron's vows, he credited his mom for raising him around enough women to understand how precious they are, how strong and how fragile. Regina glowed with appreciation at the confirmation of her hard work raising an honorable man. Joe squeezed her hand adding his agreement to her son's words.

Before long, the ceremony was over and the party began. Aaron and Sarah picked a traditional Christmas dinner, which to them was Beef Wellington, scalloped potatoes, and the works. Dessert was wedding cake and a couple favorite Christmas cookies. It was a spectacular feast and the dancing that followed was glamorous, with a rainbow of colored dresses swirling with the music. In what seemed like a blink of an eye, the day was over. Aaron and Sarah were spending the night in a hotel at the airport and leaving early the next morning on their honeymoon. The Posse gathered in the tavern of the hotel and shared memories with Regina. She was feeling nostalgic and old, and we couldn't have that. We got them to turn up the music and someone pulled out an iPod with the song Copacabana. In the tradition we started when the very first of our children got married, the Posse danced to Barry Manilow and the show girl Lola.

୶୶

My phone rang late at night. After glancing at the time, I hurried to answer. I'm always afraid a call in the night is bad news. It was Susan. Could it be her parents? Todd?

"Susan, what's wrong?" I answer the phone.

"Nothing. I'm sorry I worried you. I needed to wait until Todd was asleep before I called. I didn't want him to hear me. I have the cutest story to tell you." A cute story can't mean that someone is hurt. I breathed a sigh of relief. "Tonight, Todd got a phone call from a girl. She said she needed to ask a question about homework, but from the blush on his cheeks, I'd guess that wasn't the case. He was so nervous and kept whispering 'go away' to me. I think Todd has a crush on her!"

They grow up so fast. Just yesterday Todd thought girls had cooties. Today he has his first crush. Tomorrow Susan will be helping him with the seating plan for his wedding. When did time start flying by?

"Jules, are you there?"

"Yes, I'm here. I drifted off to Todd's wedding for a minute. Sorry."

"Slow down! He has his first crush. We have a lot of firsts to get through before we start planning his wedding." I guess in the years since Susan became Todd's mother, she hasn't realized how time flies by. She spent so much time becoming a family with him, and now that they are starting to feel like they've been a family forever, they will start to notice. Before long, he'll have been with her for half his life, then more than half. Then he'll ask her what she remembers about Jenny, because he won't remember anything in particular.

They are so lucky they have each other. They are a family!

☙❧

I got a call this morning from a number I hadn't seen in a long time. It was my old boss' boss Simon calling from my old company. I could hear the question in my voice as I answered the phone, "hello?"

Turns out they had a big shake up at work. I got the run down from Simon. After I got laid off, I purposely severed all my ties with the place. I wanted to move on. I didn't want to waste any energy on the office politics and gossip that I was lucky enough to no longer be a part of. I wanted a clean break and that's what I got.

After I left, the whole place went to "hell in a hand basket", to quote Simon. They spent the first six months after I left trying to figure out why everything was falling apart. Then the next six months trying to figure out how they'd all been hoodwinked by my boss. The third six months were spent getting enough evidence to get rid of him. The last six months were spent surviving and figuring out how to entice me back.

I laughed out loud! Really? It took them two years to figure out what went wrong and how to fix it? I know the wheels of corporate America turn at a snail's pace, but two years? Seriously? I can't imagine business moving that slowly. I want to work for a fast paced organization and have a good boss. I'm delighted to say, that's what I have right now as a self-employed person in a company of one.

"Are you calling to tell me I was right? You know I was right. Don't you? All those years you tried to console me by saying our management styles were just different. Are you ready to admit now that you knew he was a self promoting jerk all along?"

He sounded exasperated "You and he never saw eye to eye. You wanted different things from your careers and went after them differently. In the long run, your style was better suited for the organization and I should have supported you more. I understand now that the only reason he got rid of you was to eliminate his competition. He would have succeeded if someone else came behind you to do his job without recognition or appreciation."

"I'm sorry. I can't work for an organization that took two years to figure out that what I was telling them all along was true. You could have faced the facts years ago and made the right choice then, but you didn't. I can't work there again. I will never give so much time and energy to an organization that is that easily manipulated. I'm truly sorry it took you this long to figure it out. Honestly, even if you came to me the next day, I would have given you the same answer." At least I hope I would have.

After we hung up I was elated! I was just offered a great job and I turned it down. Because I could. That was completely exhilarating.

I also realized that we had talked for almost an hour and he never said he was sorry about what happened. Simon was in charge, but he never took responsibility for the actions of my boss. I don't miss the corporate world. I don't miss it at all!

Chapter 7
Exploring the World

None of us can believe we are actually there! The Winter Olympics are about to begin and we are sitting in the American cheering section waiting for the opening ceremonies. Over the past thirty years, we had watched some of the Olympics together, especially eager to watch the opening ceremony. Here we are in Sochi, Russia watching the opening ceremony wearing our American flag hats with our red parkas and blue mittens. It is cold in Sochi! I can't believe people live here.

"Remember how long these ceremonies seemed before we had TiVo to speed through the boring parts?" I asked. Frankie nudged me. He was afraid Lauren would think I was complaining and that I'd hurt her feelings.

"I know", Lauren agreed "and at least at home we aren't freezing out butts off and the bathroom is convenient." We all agreed with her, especially about the bathroom. We still didn't know where many of the countries were, but Shamus had his iPhone out with a world map so he could provide rough geography. As quickly as the next country was located, we forgot where the previous one was.

We know America has 122 athletes competing this year. We wondered how we would ever pick Russell out in the crowd. Shamus told us about Russell's plan to be picked out from the pack. "He said he'd be walking near Shawn White. They became good friends once Russell stopped his hero worshiping of the guy. Shawn's red hair is his trademark and easy to spot from a distance. To be sure we didn't miss him, Russell said he'd take off his hat every hundred steps and swing it over his head". We should notice that. If all else fails, I have binoculars.

We had been in Russia for a week already. We knew once the games began, we would want to stay close to the action, so we did our sightseeing beforehand. The country was so old, the architecture told many stories. Americans don't understand history until they travel to places that are really old, and Russia is really old.

We are staying here for another week to see Russell's competitions. Once he's done, we are separating. Frankie and I are going to Paris. He promised me we'd go there together one day and what better time than the present? Lauren and Shamus are going on to China for two weeks. Regina and Joe are heading to Italy, some little villa they hadn't been to yet. Aimee and Susan are heading to do some spelunking in New Zealand. I could never go spelunking. They travel the world looking for bigger, deeper, more exciting caves to explore. I get scared just listening to their stories!

After the ceremony finishes, we go searching for Russell. Lauren and he determined a location to meet before the festivities began, but he isn't there. We order a round of champagne to toast him and wish him luck and he arrives just as the cork is released. "Here's to winning the gold",

Shamus toasts. Here, here! Russell modestly says he'll settle for finishing and not embarrassing himself or his country. We are wishing for a much better standing for him. After just a sip, Russell bids us good night and goes off to his room to get a good night sleep. He's not competing tomorrow, but he wants to build up his stamina.

The next day, we met in the restaurant early enough to get a quick breakfast before heading to watch the competition. Since Russell isn't competing today, we decide to go look for an event without a huge crowd. We settle in to watch some of the skeleton practice runs. "Remember in 2010 when that guy went off the track in practice and died?" Shamus asked. There's a memory I could have done without today. We spent a couple hours watching the men practice. It is unbelievable how fast they go and how little protection they have in case of an accident. After hours of watching, our nerves have given out and we are freezing. The Posse decides to go look for hot chocolate and the men go look for cognac. We decide to meet up in a couple hours.

In our search, we find out about a hot tub nestled into the side of a mountain on the other side of our resort. We decide to go get our swimsuits and enjoy hot chocolate spa-side. Nothing like getting warm from the inside and the outside! We have a leisurely time in the tub then decide we better go back to our rooms to get ready for dinner. You wouldn't believe how hard it is getting out of a hot tub in the freezing cold. Now we know why we were the only people in the tub! The joy of being in it quickly dissolves as the water on your body turn to ice.

Russell would be practicing tomorrow and competing the following day. At last, the wait is over. This is what Russell has been driving towards for his entire life. This is what Lauren and Shamus were willing to separate the family for. This is the moment. The family sacrifice is about to be put to the test. We are all incredibly nervous for Russell.

Russell doesn't join us for dinner. He decides to spend the evening with his coach and teammates. They are all excited and nervous about practice tomorrow. Everyone gets six runs. Six minutes. That's it.

Frankie got me a telephoto lens for my camera. He knows that Lauren always depends on me for pictures and he didn't want me to let her down. I planned to stand on my seat if I have to, anything to get that perfect shot! Well, anything as long as it doesn't land me in a Russian prison.

At last the practice begins. We are on pins and needles waiting to hear Russell's turn announced. We know this is practice, but it can be a confidence builder or breaker. His first run he gets a tough break and falls on this second rotation. The snow looks icy. Knowing the terrain will help him do better on the next try.

His second try is much better. He finishes but scores lower than we hope. We want to yell Boo to the judges, but we don't want to get Russell any bad attention. He falls again on his third run, just over half way through it.

Russell nails his fourth, fifth and sixth runs. Each one gets better! Shawn White is really excited and keeps pumping Russell up. If Shawn thinks Russell could be a contender, then who knows, maybe he could.

At last the Americans are done their practice runs. It's time to go see a little bit of the city. The Olympic committee set up many sightseeing options and we are going to see the City of Lights tonight. Again Russell opted out. He is taking Carter to a party with a bunch of the athletes. Carter is looking forward to meeting everyone and has an autograph book tucked in his pocket. I doubt he'll pull it out, even though he's hoping to use it to score dates with girls back at college. We'll see. His friends might be more amazed to see him front and center greeting Russell after each run on international television.

The next morning, we are up and ready before the sun. We need to get to the stadium early enough to get seats and plan to spend the entire day there. It will be a long day, with lots of waiting between very short moments of high anxiety and hopefully enormous amounts of glee!

I couldn't figure out exactly how the elimination worked, but after a long morning of competition, Russell made it to the finals! We were stomping our feet and screaming "U S A. U S A!" at the top of our lungs. After all his hard work, Russell is a medal contender. I sure hope someone is TiVo-ing this at home.

The finals begin in an hour. That isn't enough time to go get lunch, besides we don't want to risk losing our seats. We pass the time looking at the photos I took. More than one of them show Russell airborne. In one you can see his face clear as day, and he has a calm demeanor that looks almost spiritual. I can't wait to get prints of that one. Lauren should use it in the news letter update she'll be sending to all of Russell's sponsors.

As the music changes, we hear the Olympic melody begin. More camera crews have assembled indicating it's the final heat of the competition. The United States has five competitors in the finals, one more than last time. Coming into the finals, Sean White is still the man to beat, and Russell has a chance. If he can land all his tricks perfectly, he could win a medal. We are dying here. Lauren can barely even watch. Russell will be competing 7th out of 12.

By now, we have all become experts at judging. "He missed that landing" Joe shouts. Susan follows with "he missed half a twist there." We are all nervous and just trying to get through the wait. Russell is up next. I stand up and aim the camera. I am going to watch through the screen on the camera, hoping that will remove me enough to let my heart keep beating. He's off, and what a start! Each second seems like minutes. He is flying so high, twisting so clean, and moving so efficiently. It's like a dance on a snow board. When he lands the final jump, he knows he nailed it. So does the crowd and we all go wild! He is attacked by his teammates, all jumping in a pile like school boys. The seconds tick on before the score is posted... and Russell is in first place!

With five more competitors remaining, Russell is in first place. Amazing! Shawn still has to go, but maybe he's past his prime and Russell will keep the lead. I can barely watch.

When the last snow boarder is done, Shawn White takes the Gold, Russell takes Silver and I have no idea who got the Bronze. What an adventure! Our adrenaline is waning and we are crashing but we can't leave before we see the medal presentation and get to congratulate Russell in person. What an amazing trip this has been for all of us!

Even though Russell won the Silver medal, we got the pleasure of hearing the Star Spangled Banner played. It was played for Shawn White who won the Gold, but we all felt like it was played for Russell. What an amazing event, definitely something we'll never forget.

Lauren and Shamus plan to host a celebration dinner tonight. After tonight, some of us will start leaving. Only Russell is staying for the closing ceremony. The rest of us will scatter the globe then regroup back at home in a couple weeks.

Frankie and I are leaving in the morning for Paris. I know it will be too cold to enjoy the outside cafes, but I hope we can find other ways to entertain ourselves. I am looking forward to seeing Paris all lit up from the top of the Eiffel Tower. I'm hoping the reflection of the lights on the snow will be spectacular! Strolling the halls of the Louvre could be spooky since I expect far fewer people there than last time I visited. This will be Frankie's first time in Paris and I want to be sure it's memorable for him.

Lauren and Shamus are heading to Beijing for two weeks. Shamus has been there for work and has marveled at the sites. He wanted to share them with Lauren, and since they are most of the way there, they decided to make this a long overdue second honeymoon. Actually, they have made full use of the Posse's babysitting services while the twins were little and they have had quite a few 'second' honeymoons. So many actually, that we've stopped counting. As much as Frankie and I are looking forward to seeing their pictures, we really have no desire to go there. We are too old and too spoiled to rough it on vacation. At this point in our lives, all we want is to be spoiled.

Regina and Joe leave right after us. They are going to Tuscany, Italy. They have both been to Italy before, but never together. What a romantic ending to a first vacation. Regina and I chatted last night. Joe had a great time with the guys. I'm so happy he fits in. Introducing suitors to the Posse is always a challenge and must be intimidating to the men. Shamus and Frankie both welcomed Joe and they all get along like brothers – for the good and the bad of it! Aaron's also accepted Joe into his life. I'm sure Aaron's acceptance of Joe has a lot to do with seeing his mom truly happy. Regina and I searched on line for plenty of romantic strolls and side trips she can enjoy with Joe. I'm certain they will have a wonderful time!

Then we have the adrenaline sisters, Susan and Aimee. They are leaving for New Zealand tomorrow. They are going on a weeklong spelunking expedition and they won't see daylight for seven days. That is so crazy that I can't even think about it! I am really scared of caves and hate that they love them so much. This one is the deepest cave they've ever been to, and they discussed that it might be the last one they attempt. I think they are just saying that so I sleep at night. Their guide will be sending daily messages to next of kin, so I'll at least know they are alive.

It's nice to be home. After the whirlwind world tour, we all gathered for a girls-only night with the Posse at Susan's house. We love having time to sit back, eat good food and talk long into the night. We haven't done this in such a long time, so I'm sure we'll be yakking all night! Luckily Susan was able to send Todd to her parents' house. He's far too young and impressionable to be allowed to overhear our conversations!

Before we even get our coats off, Regina is flashing her hand – a gorgeous diamond ring is settled smack on her left ring finger. "I got engaged in Italy! I was so surprised I was speechless." We all know that for Regina to be speechless is quite a feat!

"Tell us all the details. Wait, let me pour drinks so we can toast first. Then you have to spill all of it!" Susan had the blender out and was ready to pour Piña Colada's which coincidently are Regina's drink of choice. Perfect for a toast to her future.

"We were on our third night in Tuscany. Joe had arranged a dinner for us in a local cottage where the wife cooks and there is only one table for guests. We were gazing out at the stars and talking about how big the world is. Joe was saying he was amazed that in a world so crowded, he was blessed to find me. I was the world to him, and he wanted to be sure I never got away. When I turned away from the stars to look at him, he was on his knee holding out this ring." At that, she held up her hand so she could admire the glittering diamond. "Of course I said yes! Then I started crying. The owners of the cottage came rushing in to be sure everything was okay. Then they started crying. It was a wonderful night."

Regina is getting married. Just wait until I tell Frankie. He had such a good time in Russia with Joe and Shamus. He was always afraid the Posse would be broken apart if the men we selected didn't get along. Frankie believes that what we have is nearly sacred and to break us up would be worse than divorce. He'll be thrilled Joe is joining that inner circle now, and so am I. Regina deserves to be happy and clearly Joe makes her happy. Of course, it means we will never see them when the Bruins are playing, but that's okay. Regina hasn't told Aaron yet. She wants to tell him in person and they are getting together tomorrow. Once we tired of wedding talk, which took a long time, we got caught up on everyone else's news.

"Since Shamus and I got back from China, I haven't felt right" Lauren commiserated with us. She looked exhausted and just run down. "The food was really different and I didn't eat much. We also had to have bottled water, which wasn't always available. I guess I could be dehydrated."

We all told our stories of dysentery we'd suffered in our travels. "Remember when Michael ate a Caesar salad in Thailand? What part of 'don't eat raw vegetables' didn't he get?" Although Aimee was very sympathetic to her son when it happened, we all giggled about it in the privacy of our hotel room.

Lauren loved the Chinese countryside, and was amazed every time she saw the Great Wall just emerge from the hills. They walked along it for miles and miles discussing the evolution of humanity, the downfall of Communism and other deep topics. "I was just dying for a conversation about flower beds or women's gowns.

Anything frivolous and mindless. I guess when you visit a country as ancient as China, you have to expect to discuss a lot of history."

"That's why I like going to Paris. It's contemporary, but you don't have to look too for the history and it's safe to drink the water and eat the food" I said, "and talk about great food! I will never tire of croissants and chocolate spread for breakfast. Starting the day with chocolate is perfect in my book!" One of the many joys of travel for me is experiencing the food. If you can't eat freely, it dampens the adventure.

"I had been to Paris before so I picked my favorite places to share with Frankie. We both wanted to spend time in the Louvre, so we did that. We spent three afternoons there, taking our time seeing everything we wanted. We took a trip up to Normandy. I had never been there and Frankie has always wanted to go. The cold, dreary day gave the beach the proper somber demeanor you'd expect for the place. Besides that, everything else about our vacation was relaxing and upbeat. Absolutely perfect! But enough about Paris, let's talk about caves!"

Aimee and Susan had an awesome trip, but I think this might have been over the top for them. The trip there was an adventure in and of itself. Flying in from Russia was half way there, but it was the easy half. By the time they got to New Zealand, they were already exhausted. Luckily they had a couple days to rest before beginning the descent. Aimee began "we left the surface early Wednesday morning and didn't emerge until the following Friday. We only traveled 41 miles in that time, but travel is much slower through a cave than it is above ground."

Susan continued, "The Bulmer Caverns are 41 miles long and 2477 feet deep. At that depth it is cold and dark. You have to wear a helmet flashlight all the time. We spent so much time on our bellies slithering through canals no taller than two feet. It's so silent, you really feel like the only thing alive in the world." I can't even think about it. I am afraid of the dark and of being underground. What would happen if the cave got flooded, if their flashlights died, or if their guide had a heart attack? See, this is why I could never, ever go into a deep cave.

"There were seven people in our group, six tourists, plus the guide. Susan and I were the only women. Our packs had to contain all the food we'd eat for the nine days plus enough water to get from one stream to the next. We needed to have bedding, enough to keep the cold of the earth from entering our bodies. If we didn't do that, we could die." Seriously, I don't understand how that is considered vacation. Where are the fruity drinks? Where are the shows and hot tubs? I am really happy Susan and Aimee have each other to vacation with and that I don't have to go with them!

Susan seems like she was really shaken up by the whole adventure. "The sense deprivation was extreme. After the second day, we had lost all sense of time. For each 24 hour period, someone was responsible to be time keeper. We had to sleep, eat and rest at regular intervals. We had to enforce a 24 hour day on ourselves by watching a clock because our bodies weren't aware of time anymore. I was scared and lonely. I think this was my last adventure. I'm a mother now and Todd depends on me. I can't take the risk that something would happen to me on a trip like that. He'd be left with no one." I was surprised to hear Susan sound like that. She had never been a defeatist; no challenge was too great for her. Something had changed. She sounded like a mom. We'd all been there. Now that the rest of our kids were all grown and out of the house, we have more freedom. I'm happy to hear Susan's maternal instinct find a reason to come out.

At long last, we are caught up, done eating and the kitchen is cleaned up. Time to call it a night. It was great to catch up with the Posse, but I'm tired and Frankie is waiting at home.

Chapter 8

A Season of Surprises

When I got home, I told Frankie all about Regina and Joe getting engaged. As I expected, he was thrilled for them both. He was also looking forward to hanging out with him and Shamus. "If you girls keep finding husbands, we'll get to have our own Men's Posse!" That would be awesome since we had always talked about living near each other as we got old and retired. If the guys all enjoyed hanging together, they won't mind picking a home near each other. We just have to figure out how to get them to approve the eye candy pool boy we fanaticized sharing in our old age!

Frankie was curious, "did you tell the girls our news? I know you weren't planning to, but I thought maybe since you were all together."

"No, I didn't want to steal Regina's limelight. She is so happy, this should be her time."

"I agree, but if you wait too long, won't they wonder why you kept it from them?"

I know he's right but I not ready to answer all the questions. I know discussing it will help formulate it better, but I'm so nervous. Which is plain stupid since the

Posse is the most supportive and genuine group of friends a person could ever have. "I'll tell them next time we are all together."

Frankie looks at me with his 'I'll hold you to that' look. I'm so sure Susan won't like the idea. She'll throw out a thousand reasons why we shouldn't do it. Half of them will hold merit, but it doesn't matter, our minds are made up.

༄༅

Regina and Joe met Aaron and Sarah for dinner after work. They wanted to hear all about Russia and Italy, which Regina told them about with enough detail to satisfy their interest, but not so much detail it delayed the big announcement. Once drinks were delivered, Regina proposed a toast, "to happily ever after!"

Aaron didn't understand and looked at his mom showing his confusion "Is someone getting married?

Regina thrust out her hand displaying the diamond engagement ring she had kept concealed up to this point. "We are", she said as she put her other arm around Joe.

"Congratulations! Mom, Joe, we are so happy for you!" Both Sarah and Aaron beamed with happiness for Regina and Joe.

Regina and Sarah began discussing all the wedding details. Was the date set? What about a location? Who would be her maid of honor? That is the easiest question to answer. "Jules will be my maid of honor. For my first marriage, I wanted to have Jules as my maid of honor, but my mother insisted I have this other friend, one I had known longer. At that point, I already knew the other friend and I were drifting apart. I was the obedient daughter and gave in to avoid the stress. We all know how that marriage ended. This time, I am going to pick, and this time, I will marry my true love and we will live happily forever." Sarah was touched by the story and happy Regina shared it. She loved her mother-in--law and hoped that she could be as strong a woman as Regina was.

While the women were chatting about wedding details, the men were reversing roles. Aaron was taking his stance protecting his mother. "I know I don't have to say this, but you better treat her right. I'm younger than you and in much better shape. I will kick your ass if you hurt her. She's been through enough pain."

Joe smiled at the protection Aaron was showing for his mom. He put his arm around Aaron and said "I'd never dream of hurting your mom. I love her with all my heart. I will do everything in my power to make her happy."

Soon their food was delivered and conversation moved off the wedding and on to grandchildren. When would these two make Regina, and now Joe, grandparents? "About that," Aaron said. "We have some of our own news to share with you."

"We are having a baby!" Sarah beamed. She told them all about buying the home pregnancy test to confirm, and then planning a special dinner for Aaron to celebrate the news. "We are three months pregnant. We don't know if we are having a boy or girl yet and we haven't decided if we want to know."

Just wait until the Posse hears. We'll be planning a baby shower and wedding at the same time. This is such exciting news.

≈≈

Lauren invited us over for a fancy dinner party. While I was thrilled to dress up, Frankie was disgusted. "Why do I have to get dressed up on a Saturday night? It's not a wedding or a funeral. This isn't fair. Just because you girls want to dress up doesn't mean the guys should have to. I'm sure Joe and Shamus aren't happy about this either." I gave him a gentle pat on the cheek. He knows how much I love to see him in a suit. He especially loves when we come home. As we are getting undressed, I always take his tie and see if we can come up with any interesting games to play with it. If I remind him of that now, we'll never get to the party.

"Lauren has been looking forward to this for a long time. She said we'd have place cards and printed menus", I said as Frankie was backing the car out of the garage. Actually, Lauren's been planning this party since the twins were four years old. They are now twenty. I guess it took getting them out of the house to give her the time to properly plan the event. I'm very excited. Excited enough to wear pantyhose and heels on a Saturday night.

We are greeted with the house all aglow with lights. Rather than go in through the garage, we go to the front door like real company. Shamus answers the door and takes our coats. He gives Frankie a corsage to put on my wrist. They've thought of everything. We are directed to the breakfast nook for appetizers and wine while we wait for the others to arrive. Regina and Joe arrive next followed shortly after by Aimee and Susan. As we're all sipping our wine and admiring our corsages, we notice a teenage girl running between the kitchen and the dining room.

"Who's that?" I whisper to Lauren when she's out of earshot. Turns out she's a co-workers daughter hired for the evening to serve our dinner. How decadent! Lauren and Shamus spent the day setting the stage and preparing the feast. Now they want to enjoy themselves like the rest of us. As Lauren settled in with her glass of wine, Shamus made a show of putting a corsage on her wrist. Lauren still isn't feeling great. They've been back a couple weeks now, you'd think whatever she caught in China would be through her by now. She's smiling, but I can see the discomfort in her eyes.

Dinner was spectacular. We talked a lot about the future. Not next year, but five or ten years from now. By then we'll all be sprinkled this side or that of sixty. We all had dreams of retiring by the time we were 40. Then 50. Now we just hope to retire before we die. Shamus and Lauren want to travel the world. They saw a lot of it before the twins were born, but haven't traveled significantly since then. We all went to Russia to see Russell compete, but there is so much more to see.

Susan wants to watch Todd set off on his own path to the future, and then she can settle in at home and have a huge garden. She wants make homemade soups and bread to give all her neighbors alongside the cookies she already gives them. She can't even think of Todd getting married and starting a family because he's still a kid. She wants to wait until he has his first real girlfriend before marrying him off!

Regina and Joe want to spend their time being Bruins groupies. They want to attend every game, both home and away. They've started planning their wedding, which is supposed to be simple, but no doubt will be spectacular! Someday soon she wants to bounce a grandbaby on her knee.

Aimee is so happy running her program and watching people gain control of their lives that she never wants to retire. She visits Michael a few times a year, and he comes up with his family about that often too. She is happy, and fulfilled.

Frankie and I are quiet. We aren't sure we are ready to tell everyone our plans. We are still trying to iron out the details ourselves. Somehow we chat about everything except our plans and no one realizes it. On the drive home Frankie asks why I didn't tell them. "They're your Posse, you need their support", he tells me. I know that, but I'm not sure I'm ready to answer their questions.

❧

I got a hysterical call from Susan this morning, something about Todd's mother and a guy she used to date. Could this be Todd's father? Jenny told Susan she didn't know who Todd's father was. His birth certificate didn't list anyone as his father. I meet Susan for coffee at The Daily Paper. Kristin had been serving us coffee for so many years she's like family. One look at Susan, and Kristin decided to serve up a crock of warm apple crisp with coffee before we even settle into our booth. Ah, the breakfast of champions!

"I got a call this morning at home. I had just put Todd on the bus and I was gathering my things to head to work. I was distracted when I picked up the phone. The guy's name is Bob something. He dated Jenny in high school. He was looking for Jenny and traced her to this area. I didn't get all the details on how he found me, but he did." Susan was distraught. I hadn't seen Susan this worked up since she first found out Jenny was leaving Todd to her.

"Do you think he's Todd's father?" I ask.

"I don't know. He said they grew up together. Jenny was sixteen when she got pregnant. It could have been a boy from her home town or from school."

"Did he ask about a child? Wouldn't you assume Jenny would have told him if she had his baby?"

"What do I know? They were kids. Todd is twelve now, they weren't much older than him."

"Are you going to meet with him?"

"Yes, we are getting together tonight for coffee right here. Will you come with me? I can't do this alone."

Susan has always been so strong and self reliant. Since she became a mom to Todd, she has realized how important her support network is and has called on us when she needs help. She's still super woman, but sometimes she needs some backup, like now. "Of course I'll be here. What time?"

I got to Susan's house in plenty of time to ride together to the diner. She was a nervous wreck. She decided she'd leave Todd home alone since we wouldn't be far or gone for long. She called the neighbor next door to ask her to be on alert. If Todd needs anything, he just has to give her a call. She'll check in with him in an hour if we aren't back yet.

I decided to drive since Susan was so nervous she'd likely crash the car. She kept asking what he could possibly want from her. What could he know about Jenny, especially since she has no family? How did he find Susan? I assured her that all our questions would be answered soon.

We got to the diner a few minutes early. It was pretty quiet this time of night so we'd have some privacy. At precisely the time arranged, a tall lanky man walked in. He had thick brown hair curling back away from his face. He wore it long, resting on his shoulders. His eyes were dark brown, so dark you couldn't see the pupils. If he was in his late twenties or early thirties, he had lived a hard life. He looked worn, worn out. "Susan?" he asked extending his hand, "I'm Bob. Bob Savin."

"Hi, I'm Susan and this is my friend Juliette. Let's sit down."

This was awkward, but if we could break the ice initially, it would be easier for everyone. "Please, call me Jules." Then I jumped right in, "so you knew Jenny? Did you grow up together?" I asked. Susan looked relieved that I took the lead.

"Yes, we lived in the same town all our lives, well until Jenny left. We went to school together and started dating when we were 14."

"That was pretty young. How did your families get along? I would think in a small town that would be important."

"Jenny didn't get along well with her parents, but my parents loved her. I was an only child and mom always hoped for a daughter. She thought she had found one in Jenny."

So far, Susan had been quiet letting me ask all the questions. "What happened?" she drove right to the heart of the matter.

"I don't know" Bob shock his head in bewilderment. "One day we were happily dating and couldn't stand to spend a minute apart. The next minute she's gone. Her parents said she went to live with an Aunt in Massachusetts who needed her help. She wouldn't give me an address or phone number. I figured if I waited a couple days, Jenny would call me."

"But she didn't?" Susan couldn't imagine loving a man and just leaving him. Even if they were only teenagers.

"No, she didn't. After a week, I went back to her mother's house and asked again. I got the same answer. I pestered them every week or so for six months. The last time I went back there, there was a moving truck in their driveway and then they were gone. I had no idea where they went. No matter how hard I searched, I was never able to track down Jenny."

Bob looked like he was going to cry and it was a look I recognized. He looked like Todd. I didn't notice the resemblance until I saw the tears in his eyes. "You loved her?" I asked softly.

"Yes, Jenny is the only girl I ever loved. Everything good that happened to me paled because she wasn't there to share it. One night on TV I saw a show advertising a private investigator to find missing people. I hired him. He led me here. I don't know what your connection is to Jenny. I only know she was living with a guy who seemed like a real loser. When pressed about her whereabouts, he said all he knew was her stuff was shipped to you. Do you know where Jenny is?"

"Jenny was living with that man. He abused her physically and emotional. She would check into a home for abused women in Boston and that's where I met her. I counseled her in resume writing and job skills and I helped her find a job and break her dependency on that jerk."

"That's great. She's very lucky she met a woman like you, Susan. I'm so glad she met you. Can you tell me where to find her? I want to talk to her."

Susan began to cry quietly. This man obviously loved Jenny, or at least he loved her at one time. She spent the last years of her life trying to feel worthy of someone's love, when all along this man was pining for her. Her mother was a monster for keeping them apart.

"Jenny is gone."

"Gone where?", Bob asked, afraid he found another dead end.

Susan began crying in earnest. I reached out for her hand and for his hand. "Bob, Jenny is dead. She died of lung cancer."

Through the tears, with fits and starts, we got the story out. We told Bob about the abuse, the trips to Alliance House, and the times Jenny returned to the jerk. "That's what she'd call him, the jerk. I'd ask her why she kept going back to that man when she couldn't even say his name. She'd just say that's what she deserves. It took years for Susan to convince Jenny that she deserved better. She was finally on the right path when she was diagnosed. Even though it's against policy for a woman to stay longer than three months, Alliance House made an exception for her. They made an exception for Todd too."

"Who's Todd?" Bob asked confused.

We told Bob about Todd. We did the math and it seems likely that Bob is Todd's father. Bob was both devastated and thrilled by that possibility.

We tried to piece together the time from when Jenny left her hometown to when she showed up at Alliance House. We assumed that her mother must have forced her to leave their small town when they discovered she was pregnant. There must have been a relative here that she came to live with. In all the years Bob had known her, she never mentioned family in Massachusetts. That makes us think it was a distant relative, or it could have been a home for unwed mothers.

From there, she had Todd and didn't give him up for adoption. That could have been what her parents expected. That might explain why they left town so suddenly after six months. Maybe they moved here to help her. Bob doubts that because they were always self centered and Jenny just didn't matter that much to them. He doesn't believe they'd have come up here for her. Whatever made them move had to be self serving.

However, that doesn't explain how Jenny could have had his child without telling him about it. He could have been there. He could have helped.

Bob wanted to know where Todd is now. Susan told him that Jenny had left her as guardian and she adopted him. Todd is legally her son now. This pleased Bob. "You seem like a very good person, a hardworking woman with strong values and morals. Todd is lucky to have you as his mother."

Susan and I were both happy he saw it that way and she thanked him for the compliment.

Bob asked if he could meet Todd. Susan said of course he could, but she needed some time to prepare Todd, and we needed to keep in mind that Todd may not be his son. The resemblance between the two was strong and Susan was too emotional to accept it. I decided it might be a good idea to have a picture of Bob to show Todd before they met. I asked Bob's permission then snapped a couple shots with my phone.

Susan and Bob agreed to talk the next day. Susan wasn't planning to discuss it with Todd tonight. She had to digest the whole story better and work out a way to tell a boy that he might have a father after all. It had been an emotional meeting and was destined to be a long night.

ॐ

Lauren is annoyed and short tempered from feeling run down for so long. "I can't believe I'm still feeling sick. We've been back from China six weeks. How could I have caught a bug that has lingered this long without getting any worse or any better?"

It's hard seeing her this way. Lauren never lets anything bother her. She is always so energetic and happy. I start to wonder... "Lauren, Aaron's wife Sarah is feeling run down too. She's exhausted all the time and often complaining about food just not agreeing with her."

"Yeah, but she's pregnant" Lauren declares then turns to me with frantic eyes. "No way, I can't be? Can I?"

We sit down with a calendar. We start counting weeks. We go back and count them again. It's very possible Lauren is eleven or twelve weeks pregnant. "I can't have a baby. I'm forty six years old. The twins are practically adults. What do I know about babies?" She signed heavily.

"Jules, I'm going to have a baby."

"Don't get too worked up. Let's go get a home pregnancy test kit. You can take it to be sure." We went to the drug store and picked one up. Lauren sat jittering in her seat for the entire drive. She was so nervous that it was practically contagious.

We got back to the house and Lauren went immediately into the bathroom. I paced outside the door like an expectant father, or in this case Auntie. I didn't know what to hope for, and more importantly, I didn't really know what Lauren hoped for. This all happened so fast. Lauren hadn't even called Shamus yet.

I can't stand the waiting anymore so I go in to the family room to sit in front of the television. Maybe that will distract me while I wait for Lauren to come out. What could be taking her so long? Finally, when I don't think I can wait a minute longer, I get up and head back to toward the bathroom just as Lauren comes out. She's holding her cell phone and tears are running down her face. "Are those tears of happiness?" I asked, nervous about how to respond.

"I am going to have a baby!" Lauren declared and she burst into tears. Tears of joy and fear combined. "I called Shamus. He said he was beginning to suspect it, but didn't want to ask. He is thrilled! I asked if he thinks we are too old and he said no. I thought he was looking forward to retiring by the time he was fifty five. That won't happen now with the baby. We'll be mid-sixties by the time the baby graduates high school, never mind college. Jules, are we crazy?"

How do you respond to that? Lauren wanted a daughter forever. Having the twins was great, but she never got her little girl. Here's another opportunity. I'm sure that's what she's thinking, but she would never say it out loud. She won't want to jinx anything and speaking the words sometimes feels like asking for trouble.

"Looks like we'll be celebrating two babies and a wedding this summer!" I am very happy my roles are maid of honor and Auntie for all events!

Chapter 9
Small Decisions, Big Impact

[Left off with Quotes here] Susan typically leaves work early on Thursdays to pick Todd up from school. They go to the library for a couple hours and then out to dinner. It became a tradition early on when Susan didn't know what kind of resources Todd would need for school work and took comfort in the advice of the librarians. Susan has long since mastered homework and projects alike, but regardless, the tradition holds. Todd enjoys the time at the library as much as Susan does and conversation over dinner is always fun. Today, Susan is planning to tell Todd about Bob.

"Todd, I have something important to discuss with you. About a week ago, a man called me. He was a friend of your mother's. They grew up together." Todd was staring at her with wide eyes. He looked terrified. Susan had no idea what he was so scared of and it broke her heart to see his fear.

"Please don't be scared. There is nothing to be afraid of."

"Is this the man my mom and I used to live with?"

"No, I will never let him near you. This is a different man. A man who knew your mother when she was young, before you were born." Susan let that sink in. It seemed to calm him down a bit.

"Did he ever meet me?"

"No Todd, he didn't. He didn't even know you were born. See your mom and he were friends as children then started to date when they got older. One day, he went to see your mom and she was gone. Her parents wouldn't tell him where she went. In six months, her parents left too. He never knew where they all went. About a year ago, he started searching. He didn't know your mom was sick or that she had died. When he traced her to me, he found out. He was devastated. He feels terrible that he waited so long to track her down and now it's too late. You see he loved your mom. A lot. I told him about you."

Todd looked up at me quizzically. He was processing it all, trying to imagine his mother as a girl, then a little older with a boyfriend. He could see her sitting at the movies holding hands with a boy not much older than him. "Why would this guy care about me?"

This is the tough part. Susan has been practicing what to say for a week. How do you tell a boy that his father might have just shown up and how will he take it? He seems to be fine with the fact that some man who knew his mother is around. Before, it was just Todd and I who remembered Jenny. Now there was a man who shared the memory of her.

"Todd, I think this man is your father. We aren't sure, but his story makes sense, if you put it together with what your mom told me."

Todd looked at me with saucer eyes. "Please don't give me to him! I don't even know him. I love you. I want to stay with you. Please don't make me leave!" Instantly Todd was crying and so was Susan. She scooted over to his side of the table and cradled him in her arms.

"Don't cry Todd. I won't ever let you go. You are my son now and no one can take you away from me." They both sniffle and dry their eyes.

"Really? You won't give me to him? What if he's bad like the man Mom ran away from? What if he hits me like that guy who hit Mom?" He was terrified of men. Terrified that men hurt people smaller than them. Susan needed to help him realize that most men are honorable people and he need not be afraid of them. If Bob does turn out to be his father, and he's worthy of it, she'd encourage him to stay in Todd's life. Be a positive role model just like Frankie, Shamus and Joe. They were all good men that Todd can learn from.

"Todd, most men aren't like that guy. Most men won't hurt you. This friend of your mother's, his name is Bob, is in town for another week. He'd like to meet you." Again Todd looked at her with fear in his eyes. "There is nothing to be afraid of. He's really nice and he loved your mother. I think you'll like him. Besides, I'll be there the whole time."

Todd agrees to meet with Bob. He will try really hard to be brave and not to be afraid. He will do it for Jenny. Susan didn't tell Todd that Bob has a bunch of pictures of Jenny when she was growing up. I'm sure Todd will love seeing them. Bob even plans to let Todd keep them. I hope it's a good meeting. Susan decides having dinner at the house will be best since Todd is comfortable there. She will call Bob in the morning to make a plan.

୨୦୧

It's seems like forever since we last got the Posse together. It's probably because so much is going on right now. Lauren is getting big! She's nearly six months pregnant and absolutely glowing! She had an amniocentesis done so the doctor knows the baby's gender. As of right now, Lauren and Shamus don't want to know. They think this is the last big surprise they will have in their life, so they want to savor it. Besides, if this is the girl Lauren has longed for, she will have eighteen years to buy her every darling outfit in the world. She really doesn't have to start now!

"I don't want a shower from you guys", Lauren said with conviction. She never liked it when mothers had showers with their second child and this is her third, so it would be that much worse.

"Lauren, it's been such a long time since you had the twins that this is like your first all over again. You need everything!" She hated to be reminded how old the twins are because it reminded her how old she was. She worried she was too old to be able to keep up with this baby.

"My biggest fear is that when Shamus and I are out with the baby that people will think we are the grandparents. That will drive me crazy!" We all laughed. It was so unlike Lauren to care about what anyone thinks. This was definitely the hormones talking. "As you cold, mean women love to point out, this baby is like my first because it has been so many years since the twins were born. If that's the case, then Regina must be a blushing, virginal bride because her first wedding was way earlier than the birth of my twins!" We all remember the roller coaster of emotions when you are pregnant. One minute you are desperate, the next exuberant. Poor Shamus.

Regina and Joe's wedding is right around the corner. She has no idea we have a shower planned for next Friday night. It is going to be a small affair, just about a dozen close friends. Since both Regina and Joe have nicely stocked homes that they'll be combining, household items really weren't necessary. To avoid getting gifts they don't need, we went with a theme. Guests are to bring a consumable product to represent a favorite part of the world. We included ideas like olive oil from Greece or bath salts from the Dead Sea. I can't wait to see how creative everyone is.

Regina wanted to talk about her wedding. It was only seven weeks away. "I went for a dress fitting and absolutely love it! It's soft pink with a very tailored top and flowing skirt. I'm sure I can cut off the bottom, hem it and wear it again." We had all seen the dress. We were all there when she found it but listened patiently to her description anyway. Her eyes danced and I swear she floated when she tried it on. If ever a dress was made for Regina, it was this one!

"Have you decided on the details of the ceremony yet?" Susan asked. Aaron would love to walk his mother down the aisle to Joe, but she didn't think she wanted that. She'd been walked down the aisle once before and that didn't turn out so well. Besides Joe asked Aaron to be his Best Man. Regina cried when Joe told her he had asked and Aaron had agreed. She was pleased that Joe would honor Aaron with that important role.

Regina decided to see what the Posse thought of her idea. "I was thinking all of you except Jules would walk down the aisle first and then take the first row of seats on the left. Then Joe and Aaron would walk in together and stand up in front to the right. Last, Jules and I would walk in together and stand in front of you guys. What do you think?"

"I love it!" I said immediately. "The tradition of one man 'giving' a woman to another man is ridiculously outdated. It is a union of a man and a woman and you'll have your closest friends and family right up front with you. Perfect!"

Everyone agreed the idea suited them completely. Neither Regina nor Joe like traditional pomp and circumstance. They had decided to write their own vows to make the ceremony as personal as possible. They had both stood up there before, but this time they were making sure they did everything the way they wanted. It was going to be a small gathering, but I'm certain they have some surprises even the maid of honor isn't aware of yet.

"When is Sarah due?" Aimee asked. She knew it was soon, but forgot exactly when.

"She's seven months along. So she's due three weeks after the wedding. She better not have that baby while I'm away on my honeymoon. We are purposely making it short so we are back in time." Regina didn't want to miss Sarah and Aaron's baby being born, or Lauren and Shamus's for that matter. She considered pushing her wedding off, but she didn't want to wait for that either. Joe suggested they take a short, local honeymoon now and save the big trip for later. Regina is always amazed at his thoughtfulness and creativity in solving these kinds of problems.

So, in the next two months, we have a shower for Sarah and Aaron that we all know about. We have a shower for Regina and Joe that Regina doesn't know about. A shower for Lauren and Shamus that Lauren doesn't know about. I'm getting too old for this!

Aimee has been so busy, she's barely has time to see the Posse anymore. She received approvals from two other insurance companies in the past week. She can now accept clients from the top three insurance providers in New England. Her boss wasn't happy to hear she got the approvals and called her in to his office to discuss it.

Aimee argued that the program at the hospital had a focus toward weight reduction surgery and not everyone wanted to go that route. He argued that surgery is where the hospital made the most money so that would be where she recommended clients. Aimee thought pushing surgery onto ill-prepared clients was unethical. They got into a huge argument. When Aimee left his office, she left without her keys. The next day, neither she nor he boss would remember if she was fired or if she quit. Regardless, they were both relieved.

Aimee invited us all over. She was cooking again, which is her classic response to stress.

"Yum! Something smells good." It sounded like a chorus when we came through the door. Aimee greeted us with a new appetizer to try, a crab and hummus salad on endive leaves. We were so busy munching that we barely heard when Aimee said "I lost my job today." She got the story out while we peppered her with questions and murmured reassurances.

"Jules, it's time to make a business out of my program. I retained copyright to the material I taught at the hospital. I don't care if they keep using it, but legally, it's all mine."

Lauren hadn't been around much so she wasn't aware Aimee was teaching outside the hospital. "Is your program like Weight Watchers?"

"A portion of it is like Weight Watchers. I teach balanced nutrition. The benefit is that I'm a registered Dietician, so I can help with specific problems individuals have. It also has an exercise component. As a personal trainer, I can help people find an exercise they can and will do I can work with them to find something they enjoy. The third component is emotional eating. This part helps you cope with the stress and triggers that cause overeating. The entire program is very successful."

As a long time Weight Watcher, Lauren was intrigued. Aimee explained that she's been running two sessions for about three months. In one session, she cycles between the three components teaching one a week. In the other program, she splits the hour and a half into three sections and touches on each area weekly. That method has shown the most success so far.

Susan, of course brings us right to point "Now that you aren't affiliated with the hospital anymore, what does that change?"

"For my clients attending the program at the hospital, I was grooming them for surgery. For the clients I was seeing outside, I was not pushing surgery. I discussed it briefly as an alternative, but I was encouraging weight loss through moderation of eating and exercise."

"Where are you meeting?" Lauren was curious, thinking about the baby weight she'd be trying to get rid of before long.

"At a local VFW hall. I rent the time and charged people what they could afford. I asked for the same weekly price of Weight Watchers, and those who can afford it, pay it. Some pay less. Others pay nothing. My main concern was that I cover the rent with what I receive. Luckily that has always worked out."

"Do you have a budget?" Susan asked. We call her our financial advisor because, well, that's what she does for all of us. Aimee explained the business plan she and I put together for her to solicit a business loan. She hadn't done much with it yet, but the time was right. This isn't going to be a big money maker, but Aimee isn't in it for the money. She wants to help people get healthy and live longer. She doesn't want to see any more lives cut short because someone doesn't have the money and insurance won't cover it.

We all settled in to a delicious meal and a low fat dessert. We all agreed that if Aimee could cook for us all the time, we would all be thin. Aimee glowed with the praise. Her confidence was restored from our praise, and she needed confidence now more than ever.

☙❧

Regina and I were having breakfast before beginning a full day of shopping. Before leaving the restaurant, I told Regina I had something to tell her. Of course, she got very concerned, fearing the worse.

"Frankie and I are moving to San Diego."

"You're kidding. Why would you move there? What's in San Diego?"

"We have always loved vacationing there and decided that at this point in our lives, we are ready to semi-retire. Since I got laid off, we've been doing fine financially. Working at Alliance House is starting to pay off through some high paying corporate sponsors. My business contracting is also picking up. Writing business plans is fun, and I love seeing someone's dream come to fruition."

"What will Frankie do?"

"He got a teaching position at UCLA. He loves UMass, but who wouldn't love UCLA? Since his research in security was published, he's been in such high demand. He used to be the only guy we knew in security, but now everyone knows someone in security. He has a dozen patents in the field and the school was thrilled to get him. He'll be teaching full time, but only three days a week. That gives us a lot of time to play!"

Regina is really sad about me leaving, but she's going to be so busy herself. Ten years ago, I was her life line, helping her through a painful divorce and the struggle of being a single mother. We spent so much time together, talking, commiserating and getting massages. Frankie would always say "another massage? You ladies are so decadent!" I'd always hit back with "we deserve it". Frankie was smart enough to agree!

Now, Regina is marrying Joe, and Aaron is giving her a grandchild. She will be so busy she won't even notice me gone.

"When will you tell the rest of the girls?" Regina asks wanting to be sure she doesn't spill my news to the Posse.

"There is so much going on right now. I'll tell them when I'm not afraid of stealing someone else's limelight." With the way things have been going this year, the Posse might not find out until they get our change of address cards! Enough about that. We need to hit the road. We have a wedding to pull together, and not much time to do it in.

Susan and Todd discussed the pros and cons of meeting Bob over and over again. Good thing they only had two days to rehash it from the time Todd learned about Bob to the night of their dinner. They covered the worst case scenario, the best case scenario, and everything in between. Todd is so afraid of losing Susan. He's experienced so much loss in his short life. He's even considered how he'll feel about losing Bob once they meet. All things considered, Todd is glad he's meeting Bob. Susan agrees it's a good decision. When the night of introductions arrives, Todd confides that he hopes Bob won't take him away from Susan.

"Todd, that won't happen!" Susan reassures him with a resolution she isn't quite so certain of. She is worried that Bob could ask for a paternity test and try to take Todd away from her. He has convinced Susan that he loved Jenny and that she loved him. If that was the case, Bob could want to have Todd around to remind him of Jenny. That would kill Susan. She may not have intended to become a mother, especially not of a ten year old boy, but she has become one, and she will protect her son with the instincts of a mother.

"Todd, Bob loved your mother. She moved away when she was sixteen and he never saw her again. He wrote her every day for a while, but after never hearing from her, gave up. He never got married and never had children. He didn't know Jenny had you."

With wide eyes, Todd asked "is he my father?"

"We don't know. Everyone who knew your mother is gone. Your birth certificate says your father is unknown. The only way to tell for sure is with a blood test. We won't do that unless you, Bob and I all decided it's the best thing to do."

"You're my mother now."

"Yes," Susan said feeling a bit choked up, "and nothing is going to change that. Now let's get going. Bob will be here soon."

ଚ୍ଛ

We're getting together tonight to surprise Regina with a small shower. We're combining her shower with a Slumber Party, an adult toy party. We'll spend two hours giggling over intimate toys then make our purchases. Unbeknownst to Regina, she will be the hostess of the party and will get ten percent of the total sales to purchase her own toys. We are all excited when we hear that the delivery date is three days before the wedding. Perfect! Then, we'll shoo everyone out and start the celebration.

The woman demonstrating the toys for the evening, first presents vibrating panties. As the hostess, Regina is required to put them on while we all hand around the remote control. We are laughing so loud that we can barely hear the product details. Somehow I don't see anyone in the Posse buying these.

The evening progresses with more products and amusing banter. "Look how big that is!", "What do you do with that?" and "You want to put that where? No way!" We tease Lauren that she doesn't need any help in the sex department. Maybe with a toy, she'd stop having babies! By the end of the two hours, we've all made our purchases, including the woman of the hour, and we were ready to begin this Bridal Shower in earnest.

As soon as the Slumber Party guest leaves, the champagne comes out. I stand up, "I want to make a toast to the bride." Regina and I have been friends longer than anyone else in the Posse. We know each other so well, and have never tired of each other.

"To Regina and Joe. May their union be blessed with happiness and pleasant surprises every single day. May they strengthen the good in one another and overlook any of their failings. May they live many happy years together and grow old in each other's arms. Let him be the man she deserves, or else the Posse will track him down and kill him!"

"Here, here!" and we all drank to Regina's happiness.

Chapter 10
New Beginnings

Aimee was able to secure a location for her program. The space will accommodate an office as well, so she could see her counseling patients. All she needs is to get the place renovated for a reasonable price. She remembered Susan mentioned that Bob was a carpenter. Aimee wondered if he was looking for some short term work.

"Susan, do you know if that guy looking for Jenny needs short term work? You said he's a carpenter, right?"

"Yes, he does finish carpentry. Why, what do you need?"

"I found a location for my offices and I need the whole thing remodeled. I want a big room we could use for meetings and exercise. I want four smaller offices for one-on-one counseling. I also want a place where clients can get weighed privately, but efficiently. A small room with two doors that people can go in one, stop at the scale and head out, without anyone seeing or hearing anyone else's weight."

"That sounds perfect. Can I come see the space? I'll bring Bob."

"That would be great. So he's still around? Do you think he'd be interested in the job?"

"Yes, he's still here. He is getting along great with Todd. They act more like brothers than father and son. Bob hasn't mentioned leaving. I don't know if he has much to go back to. He just rented a longer term place and plans to stay at least two more months. I hope after all this time he doesn't decide to leave, that will break Todd's heart. They are thick as thieves and Todd loves having him around."

Bob, Susan, Aimee and I went to the new place with property sketches and tape measures in hand. Aimee shared rough sketches of her thoughts. She had a couple different ideas and they were looking at the lighting to see how it would accommodate dividing the room. After some debate, they decide it would be best to keep the weigh in room near the offices. That way, a client wouldn't have to parade across the large room possibly interrupting a class to weigh in. The space was big enough to allow for some large pieces of equipment, like a few treadmills and stationary bikes.

"I don't want cardio equipment" Aimee insisted. "Of course I want my clients to do cardio, but I don't want them to feel dependent on a piece of equipment. I want them to understand they can exercise in the privacy of their own home without the expense of a treadmill or bike. All I need is a place for weights, some mats and some yoga balls."

Bob suggested some flooring changes for both the open space and the offices. He wanted to ensure the privacy of the office space and the durability of the floor in the open space. "Dragging chairs over the floor could scratch hardwood so a low pile industrial grade carpet would be better, but you'll want the hardwood for working out on. Let me think about how to accommodate both."

Aimee was impressed. Bob knew more than she did about renovating an open floor plan into usable business space. She was happy that she thought to ask Susan. She wondered how long he'd be around.

"Bob, could I hire you to draw up plans for the renovation? Susan said you are a finish carpenter and I need a professional's sketches to get a loan for the work."

"I'd love to. I'll do the sketches for free if you hired me for the renovation."

Well that answers the question about how long he'll be around. Too bad he wasn't older. He and Susan get along great. It would be nice for Todd if the three of them could become a family. Unfortunately, people might think Bob was Todd's brother and Susan's son. That would not go over well. I guess they will just have to be friends. I'll enjoy working with him on this project. I can't wait to see what he comes up with.

෴

Lauren went back to work shortly after returning from China. When she discovered she was pregnant, she decided to wait as long as possible before telling her boss. Not much had changed and she fell right back into her old position. Since she'd been on sabbatical, many people put off their vacations and now that she was back, Lauren found many of her colleagues taking extended vacation.

She couldn't blame them. After all, she was gone for a year.

By the time Lauren was into her eight month, everyone was gearing up for her extended absence again. After the twins were born, Lauren took six months off. She almost didn't go back at all, but the expense of twins forced her to make the sacrifice and work. She told everyone at work she'd be back in three months. Twelve weeks. She isn't really sure she'll be back. Last time it killed her to drop the babies at day care. She isn't convinced she could do it again. She and Shamus discussed all the options. In the end he said she could decide. They were financially sound and would be fine without Lauren's paycheck. The twins' college is fully funded thanks to some sound financial advice they got years ago and listened to. If Lauren wanted to stay home, she could.

She just had to decide. If she is going back, she has to find day care. It's always easier to do that before you are carrying the baby in the car seat. Thinking back to the parents she and Shamus met in various classes with the twins makes her feel really old. If she takes a couple years off, is she ending her career? Will she go back into the work force at fifty? It seems the decision is harder this time, more permanent. Try as she might, Lauren really can't imagine that she and Shamus were planning to retire once the twins were out of college. That certainly won't be happening now. Now they'll be bouncing a baby on their knees and repeating all the fun things they did with Carter and Russell.

ॐॐ

At long last, the day has arrived. Regina looks stunning! "I'm getting married today to the love of my life, a man who loves me with all his heart and loves my son like his own." There is no surprise that we both have tears in our eyes.

"Regina, you need to stop this! We have to get our makeup on and we can't do that with tears in our eyes."

"You're right. I'll stop. I am just so happy."

We had a big pajama party in the bridal suite last night with the whole Posse. We watched movies and then talked late into the night, long after the lights went out. We knew we could sleep in this morning, so it wasn't a problem for any of us. We planned a late breakfast, and then it was back to the suite to get our hair and makeup done.

None of the men had seen us since last night. Shamus, Frankie, Todd and Aaron took Joe out for dinner and to shoot some pool. Todd isn't old enough to go to a place that serves liquor, so there was no chance everyone would try to get Joe wasted. Bob ended up joining them and they all got along great. They turned in much earlier than the Posse did, and would take a great deal less time getting ready. Joe was getting nervous and needed somewhere to go. Bob decided they should go over to Aimee's clinic space and take some measurements. It would pass the time and keep Joe's nerves at bay.

Back in the suite, the Posse was having a great time. After breakfast, we went to the Jacuzzi for a while to relax before getting dressed. If only we'd thought to have a masseuse come. That would have been perfectly relaxing!

Two women arrived to help with our hair and makeup. Regina may be the star of the day, but we will be walking beside her, reflecting her elegance with our subdued beauty. Before we knew it, the limo had arrived and it was time to go. Regina began to show some jitters, but we had no time to indulge in nerves at this point.

Although Regina and Joe planned a non-traditional entrance, they conformed to the tradition of not seeing each other before the ceremony. After all the guests were seated, soft music began to play. First, the Posse's men plodded down the aisle, a gangly group comprised of Shamus, Frankie, and Todd. They choose to wear simple dark suits, with brilliant white shirts and ties that coordinated with the Posse's outfit. It amused Regina to think that to the guests assembled, they looked like odd collection of random men meandering in.

Lauren, Aimee and Susan sauntered gracefully down the aisle, arm in arm with their joy for the couple apparent on their faces. Lauren was wearing a navy blue sleeveless sheath with a plunging back and a lace bodice. Her signature blond curls were gracefully skimming her back. She hoped people would be looking at her sculpted arms and voluminous hair and not her belly. Aimee selected a blue and green flowered dress that flowed down her finely toned body and made every woman assembled wish they had gone to the gym that morning. Susan was wearing a hunter green A-line dress with a slit up to there, showing off her shapely legs to the delight of the men. Everyone assembled at the wedding knew the Posse. They could tell our friendship was so extraordinary and just being near it made others feel special. Once the girls made their way down the front, the music changed.

Joe and Aaron were waiting in a small side room. Joe was wearing a tux, his own tux. Regina enjoyed attending fancy events and getting dressing up so much that he decided to purchase a tux. Regina spent so much time debating what tuxedos they should wear for the wedding that he decided that would be the one he bought. He looked like he walked straight of the pages of GQ in his black on black striped tux with black cummerbund. Aaron was wearing the same suit as the groomsmen and looked more mature than his twenty eight years. Both men wore ties that coordinated with their Posse woman, Regina.

Joe and Aaron couldn't see the others walk down the aisle but they heard the music begin, the guests murmuring greetings as the time for the grand entrance grow closer. Aaron is playing the part of best man, father of the bride and son, all rolled into one, alternating between keeping Joe calm and fighting his own nerves. The time had arrived. With a pat on the back, Aaron said "let's go!" and off they went.

Aaron and Joe walked down the aisle side by side. Their journey was slower than anticipated due to all the congratulatory greetings guests were making. Joe beamed with joy and later that day would admit to not remembering a single soul he saw on that short walk. At times, Aaron would place his hand on Joe's back to give him a nudge forward. If they didn't make it to the front soon, the food at the reception would get cold.

Once they were all assembled up front, the music changed again. Michael Taylor was setting the mood for the grand entrance,

There's something in the way she moves or looks my way or calls my name,
That seems to leave this troubled world behind...

Regina and I had been waiting the in room opposite Joe. Regina is the picture of grace, beauty and love. She is marrying her soul mate with her eyes wide open to his flaws, as well as her own. She loves him in spite of, or maybe because of each of them. She is anxious to begin that walk to join hands with her love.

As we enter through the rear doors, the sun catches on the glittering clips in Regina's hair and the room dances with rainbows. Warm laughter breaks out as the guests marvel at the colors and pinpoint the source to the bride. Regina is wearing a soft tea rose pink dress with a silver beaded bodice and a flowing skirt. Light reflects off her sequined dress, her shoes, and her jewelry causing sparkles that enhance the joy radiating in her eyes and from her smile. Everyone stares at Regina as she glides down the aisle towards Joe. For Regina and Joe, they are the only two present. The rest of us don't matter at all in this moment, and that is perfect.

Their vows express their gratitude for each of us, their closest of friends, and for the Bruins. If it weren't for their mutual love of the Bruins, they would never have met. They wrote them together, each taking turns, back and forth, until they were perfect. Their words were so private and intimate that I felt honored to bear witness to this glorious event. By the time the official proclamation of husband and wife was made, there was not a dry eye in the place. We all needed a quick make up check before heading to the reception.

At the reception, we were surprised to see that Regina and Joe had presents for each of us. Not just us, the Posse, but every guest had a present selected just for them. Each present was a perfect reflection of what that person meant to the couple. Frankie opened his gift to find an iPod. Frankie was always listening to Joe and offering advice. Joe picked an iPod to symbolize the sympathetic ear and to give Frankie something he could listen to without having to offer advice. Regina gave me a white gold heart locket engraved "I am... Because of You". When I read the inscription, I gave Regina a tight hug and we both cried. She had weathered the storm and finally come out to thrive in the sunshine.

Regina and Joe graced the dance floor waltzing to Michael Bolton singing 'Once in a Lifetime". They couldn't have picked a song better suited or a dance more elegant. Again, we felt like voyeurs watching a private moment shared between lovers...

> Once in a lifetime, you find the one you really love
> For now and forever, one love that never ends

Regina had her favorite Chinese restaurant cater the reception, and the hors d'oeuvres being passed made mingling much easier. There were only 46 guests and Regina and Joe were able to visit with each as they opened their gifts. I had never been to a wedding where I felt so honored to be a guest.

After we all had our fill, we danced the night away to music of the '80s. Madonna sang her heart out, along with Cyndi Lauper, Michael Bolton and Survivor to name a few. Regina and Joe graced the floor with their ballroom dancing skills to the envy of all the women, and the annoyance of all the men. Of course no wedding is complete without the Posse dancing and singing along with Barry Manilow and his Showgirl Lola. In what seemed like a blink of an eye, the cake was cut, final dances completed, last hugs bestowed and the newlyweds were on their way.

It's been an absolutely perfect day. Let's toast to this being the first of many in their life together. I'll drink to that!

ಌ

It's been a busy spring and before I knew it, it was time to start thinking about wrapping up at Alliance House. In the past two years, I have developed a program to build the client's self esteem, create resumes, conduct job skills training and interview practices. I also hosted clothing drives to gather professional clothing to further boost their confidence on interviews. The program has been an unprecedented success and I'm extremely proud of my accomplishments. Since Frankie and I decided to move to the west coast, I've been training my replacement.

The woman taking over is one of the very first women I helped find a job. She arrived here in the middle of the night just two and a half years ago. She was battered and helpless, but not broken. She felt unworthy of any attention I paid her, so I worked with her initially to help build her self worth. Before long, she was looking forward to getting a job. We worked together on her resume and practiced interviewing. She landed a job with a temporary agency doing clerical work in offices around the city. She learned proper business behavior and regularly advanced within the agency. After two years with them, she was offered a permanent position. When she told me, I asked her not to take it and instead to consider working for Alliance House. She was thrilled at the opportunity. She had been volunteering two nights a week, so she was familiar with both sides of the process at Alliance House. Next month, she will begin running the program on her own. I'm so proud of her, and happy to have been a part of this remarkable woman's growth. Her success gives me one less thing to worry about once I leave here.

Marie and I got together for lunch and margaritas this afternoon. She's still unhappy that we are moving across the country, but is trying to look at the bright side. She complains that we never have enough time to together and whenever we are together, she has to share me.

"Now when we are together, it will be just us," I remind her when I see she's looking particularly glum.

"I know, but how often will that be? I don't have much time off from work and it will cost so much to fly across the country all the time."

"Marie, I won't be working a 'real' job out there, so I'll have plenty of time off. Frankie will be teaching part time so we'll come back east often. We'll also have you and Adam out to visit us. You'll see, it will probably work out better than it is now." I honestly believed this. At this point in my life, I want to be sure the time I spend with the people I love is quality time. I want to make every moment count. Working with the women at Alliance

House has taught me that life is fragile and too short to let any unhappiness move in.

Chapter 11
The Bonds that Bind Us

"I can't stand it another minute. I'm huge!" Lauren declares as she wedges herself into the booth at the Daily Paper. We met for breakfast before doing some final shopping for the nursery. Little does she know we'll be heading to a surprise shower for her and won't get much shopping accomplished.

"Of course you're huge. You are having a baby in six weeks and not just any baby, you are having my adorable niece or nephew".

"Don't you think if I'm forced to do this again, I should finally get my girl? Seriously, why give me another boy? Don't tell Shamus I said that! I told him I really don't care what the baby is."

"Shamus isn't stupid. You have been wishing for a daughter for twenty years. Why would anyone, especially your husband expect you to change that desire now? You are supposed to be moody and unbearable when you are in the final stages of pregnancy. No one expects you to be demure and understanding."

"No one's ever called me 'demure' before."

"And no one's calling you understanding right now", I said under my breath.

"I heard that", Lauren chided back.

We talked about her leave from work. It begins in four weeks, two weeks before her due date. I asked what her plans are for going back.

"Prior to becoming pregnant, Shamus and I were planning to retire in four years. By then, Carter will be two years out of school and Russell will be just finishing up. Now, in four years, we'll be thinking about kindergarten. If I don't go back to work shortly after the baby is born, I'll be fifty and looking for a job. I don't want to be retired and raising a child. The time to do that was with the twins. Having one to chase should be way easier." Of course Lauren is a lot older now, but I didn't mention that.

After breakfast, we set off to begin shopping. We went to Babies R Us first because we knew their selection would be greatest. Lauren wasn't planning to buy anything here just yet, she wanted to see what was available and use this as her fall back. Selections would be much easier if Lauren and Shamus knew what they were having, but even though she had amniocentesis, they still wouldn't find out. This made shopping much more difficult.

When we left Babies R Us, I wanted to swing past my house to pick up some fabric samples I forgot. I told Lauren we could make curtains and a crib set if we didn't find anything. Obviously Lauren knew by 'we' I meant 'me', so she readily agreed. I had no fabric at the house. Instead, I had two dozen women, friends, family and co-workers of Lauren ready to shower her with gifts and warm thoughts. She'll kill me later.

☙❧

Regina and Joe got back from their honeymoon last night. They spent a week in the Finger Lakes in upper state New York. Since Sarah and Aaron's baby is due soon, they didn't want to go far and be dependent on an airline ticket to get back. They convinced themselves and the kids that they had the rest of their lives to see the world, but only one chance to see their grandbaby born.

"We had a wonderful time! There's something magical about visiting a place together for the first time" Regina gushed. Yes, I do believe she is gushing.

"Tell me all about it."

"We stayed in a bed and breakfast that overlooked a lake. We had a private balcony and could watch the sun rise there."

"You were up to see the sun rise?" I wonder what kind of honeymoon gets you out of bed and out on the balcony watching the sunrise.

"We couldn't stay in bed all the time. Some morning we caught the sunrise after waking up bright and early. Other mornings, we caught it right before heading to sleep." Regina had a gleam in her eye that made me so happy for her. I really like Joe and he makes Regina so happy.

"Okay, so you spent time in bed and on the balcony. You must have done something else? You were gone for a week. Four walls get boring after a week, even for two starry eyed lovers like you guys."

"Of course, but I didn't think you'd care about that" Regina said with a giggle. "We took long scenic drives. The chef at the inn packed us a picnic lunch most days and we'd drive until we came across a lovely spot and stop to eat. We also spent one day at the outlet mall buying more stuff than we would ever need. Joe loves to cook and likes gadgets, fancy things that I wouldn't know how to use. We got lots of those. I am looking forward to tasting some magnificent dinner prepared with those tools!"

That sounded fun. Frankie and I love going to outlet malls too. We consider it a game to talk each other into buying things. We both play so hard that we often go home without buying anything. Then we'd berate ourselves for not buying that thing we wanted really badly until we go back again. Then we do the whole thing again only to buy nothing. We'll see how Regina and Joe's outlet shopping evolves.

Regina is ready to turn her focus away from being the bride and on to being a grandma. I'm curious what she'll want to be called. She is certainly too young to be considered a rocking-chair bond granny!

"What do you want to be called?" When the twins were little, I was dubbed 'Auntie Green Beans'. Carter had a funny way of saying two syllable words and somehow Juliette sounded green beans, and it stuck. When they were teenagers, they shortened it to 'Beans' to avoid embarrassing themselves around their friends. When I became a grandmother, my kids tried to make me 'Grandma Beans' but that didn't stick. I became 'Gee Gee', which suites me just fine.

Regina is thrilled that Aaron is having a baby, but not so thrilled about becoming the stereotypical Italian grandmother. "I feel far too young to be someone's grandmother. I mean look at me? I am so much younger than I ever remember my grandmother being."

"Yes, but your mother didn't think your grandmother was that old."

"I guess you're right. Aaron called my mother 'Gramma'. I could stick with that. It's traditional, or I could go with something different."

"How about 'Nonna'? It's a traditional Italian grandmother. What could possibly suite you better?"

Regina was delighted! That's what her mother called her grandmother. She hadn't even remembered that until this very moment. What a wonderful nod of respect to the generations. She'd be sure to ask Aaron and Sarah if that's okay with them.

Unlike Lauren and Shamus, Sarah and Aaron know they are having a boy. They wanted to know so they could be well prepared for the big arrival. Regina spoiled them rotten, getting everything the child would need straight through the toddler years. She didn't leave much for the rest of us to get.

At this point, all the parents to be were ready and waiting patiently for their babies to arrive.

ೂೊ

Susan is thrilled that Todd and Bob are getting along great. "We are all gingerly walking around the question of paternity, when it comes up. We told Todd that Bob and his mom dating when they were in school before he was born. He asked Bob directly 'Are you my father?'"

I am impressed with Todd's directness. When he wants an answer, he asked the question, even if it's tough. I wonder if it's because of all the loss he's suffered. If it doesn't get asked straight away, the person could be gone before he gets a chance. "What did you both say?"

"I tried to jump in, but Bob was too quick. Bob said he didn't know. He said 'I know that you know how babies are made, and your mom and I were doing that.' I cringed when he said that but Todd didn't. Todd just nodded his head. Bob continued 'when your mom left, I considered it might be because she was going to have a baby, but it didn't make sense to me that she wouldn't call me.' Bob looked like he would be crushed by the memory and loneliness he felt at the time."

"It must be hard for Todd to understand any of it. He doesn't really know what love feels like. He only knows what being left feels like, the poor kid."

Susan nodded. She and Bob have discussed doing the test but even they aren't sure that the benefit outweighs the risk. Bob wants to stay in Todd's life but doesn't want custody. He'd rather be something more like an uncle. Susan is so relieved that she doesn't have to worry about Bob trying to take Todd away from her that she loves the idea of Uncle Bob. "I'll even let Bob be the Favorite Uncle!"

"Make sure you are good with him being the 'take Todd for a week while the Posse goes on vacation' Uncle!" We both laugh at that. So true, so true!

❧❦

With sketches and ballpark figures in hand from Bob, Aimee began peddling her idea to banks to secure a loan for construction. She was able to generate interest in the program by showing her current success at the hospital. The insurance approvals also helped.

Before long, she had three institutions who agreed to the conditions she was looking for. All three were local banks that prided themselves on investing in the community. This was a perfect investment for them.

That night, the Posse got together at the space she planned to rent and reviewed Bob's plans one last time before Aimee committed to both the space and the loan. Aimee had worked through all the numbers. She expected construction to take five weeks. During that time, she would advertise the program at housing locations for seniors and the disabled. She would also take out a few ads in local newspapers. To pay the rent and the loan, she would have to be at one-third capacity. She could afford to be less than that for eight months. Hopefully by then, she'd be at greater than that and begin taking a paycheck.

We went out for dinner after reviewing the space and the loan contracts. Aimee was exhausted, but it was that nice exhaustion from hard work.

"I want to thank each of you for helping me realize my dream. At times, I didn't even know that this was what I wanted. It has been such a long, convoluted road but you stuck with me through it all."

"There was no way you were ditching us for this adventure" Susan said. "Who would give us free nutrition advice and all those recipes?"

Lauren laughed "Forget the recipes, who would cook for us?"

At that we all raised our glasses and drank to Aimee. It had been a long road from her high tech days managing a call center. Here she was, a registered dietician about to open her own wellness clinic.

༺༻

Susan is happy, truly happy for the first time in as long as she can remember. She has a son who loves her. A son that came to her through non-conventional means and melded together with her personality in a way that made you think they were together from the start. Todd is a bright, intellectual young man who loves technology, science fiction and museums. I doubt he was exposed to any of them prior to his biological mother's death but today you would think he was raised immersed in them.

Todd fills up a space in Susan's heart and home that was long empty. A space that needed a little boy's finger prints messing things up a bit. Susan may be a little bit disheveled around the edges now, but the look is good on her. The happiness in her eyes is there for everyone to see. She doesn't have to 'borrow' that maternal feeling from anyone else now. She has it herself. Both she and Todd are lucky. As lucky as you can be when you lose your mother far, far too young.

In spite of her happiness, there is something bothering Susan. She's staring intently at her coffee and not listening to what I'm saying. "Then the green monster sat next to me and asked for half my sandwich", I said to prove my point that she isn't listening.

"Ah huh," she said.

This is bad. What could be distracting her so much? "Earth to Susan? What's going on? You just listened to me tell you a monster joined me for lunch, and you didn't ever bat an eyelash. What's wrong with you?"

Susan looked at me with worry in her eyes. I couldn't tell if it was worry about something that she was about to do or worry about something she had already done.

"Spill it Susan."

"Bob is moving in with me. Us. Moving in with us. Yes. Bob is moving in with us." I didn't see that coming. "Really? What does that mean? Todd's dad, or uncle, is moving in with you as a roommate? Or..."

"Yes, that's exactly what it means. Bob has been living in a month-to-month rental and he wants to stay. He wants to be with Todd, to see him grow up, to be there as a positive male role model in his life. I think that's a great idea. Todd needs stability and if Bob stays, he doesn't have to lose someone else."

"So he's staying for Todd? He's going to live in your house, with you, to be a good role model for Todd."

"I know what you're thinking", Susan said with annoyance. I know she isn't annoyed with me. She's annoyed with the situation and that whatever I ask, other people will be thinking. She knows she needs to be sure this is what she wants.

"How will dating work?" I ask.

Susan laughs a sarcastic laugh. "That won't be an issue for me. I don't think I've been on a date since before Todd was born." We both know that was an extreme exaggeration. Susan is a very successful woman and tends to scare men away. When she does start dating someone, it doesn't seem to last very long. Since she's been a mother, she has avoided bringing anyone home. She doesn't want Todd to be afraid he'll be replaced.

"I know you haven't brought any dates home since you and Todd have become a family, but you do date occasionally. What about Bob? What's his dating pattern like? You don't want Todd to be bumping into any bimbos on the way to the bathroom at night."

Susan visibly cringed at the thought. "I don't want Bob bringing any bimbos into my house. He will have to spend the night at his bimbo's house. If he has a bimbo. Then what would Todd think if he doesn't come home at night. Where will Todd think he's sleeping? I guess I better discuss this with Bob, and quickly since he's moving in this weekend."

I do believe Susan is flustered. It's great to see since she's always in such cool control. If I'm not mistaken, I would say Susan has a crush on Todd's father. I don't think I've ever seen her this discombobulated.

"One benefit of having Bob around is that you won't have to worry about working late and having Todd home alone."

"You know, I haven't been working late at night much lately. I usually have breakfast with Todd, and then drop him at school. He has sports after school, and then I pick him up. I might catch up a little bit at night when Todd's doing his homework, but not often. I've discovered that moderation is the key. I do what is absolutely required then I delegate or minimize the rest. I've been slowly doing this since Todd came to live with me, and nothing has exploded. The world hasn't stopped revolving because I'm not working 60 hours a week. I wish I could have done this years ago."

"I'm so proud of you for doing it now! Susan, you are a wonderful Mom! Todd is so lucky to have you. Now he'll have his dad. I think things are working out better for him than he could have ever expected. Jenny must be looking down here missing her little boy desperately but as content as possible at her decision to leave him with you."

As expected, I got the call in the middle of the night. How come these things never happen during the day, when everyone is up and available?

"Jules, I just got a call from Aaron, they are heading the hospital. Sarah's contractions are six minutes apart. I'm going to be a grandmother!" I look at the clock. When the phone rang, Frankie grunted and rolled over. It's 4:37 am. "You go," I tell her, "I'll be along shortly."

"Okay. I'll see you when you get there. I haven't called anyone else yet."

"No problem, Nonna, I'll let everyone know." I'll hold off until after the sun rises, but she doesn't need to know that right now.

I get out of bed careful not to wake Frankie. He'll know where to find me when he rouses himself later. I take a long shower, knowing that this will likely be my only quiet time of the day. After getting dressed, I pull three loaves of sweet breads from the freezer. I made them about a week ago, knowing Sarah would go into labor in the middle of the night and we'd all be at the hospital looking at the vending machines wishing we'd stopped to get food on the way in. I'll replenish my stash next week to be sure I'm ready for when I get the call from Shamus about Lauren.

Within an hour of Regina's call, I leave the house. One stop on the way for a box of coffee from Dunkin Donuts and I'll be on my way. I'm sure I won't miss the big event since this is Sarah's first. The first baby is always slower to make their appearance.

Regina is a bundle of anxiety, nerves, and excitement. Joe is amused with her, but unsure how to handle her energy. He's relieved when he sees me come in, though he's a bit disappointed to see I don't have Frankie with me.

"Where's Frankie?" Joe asks in a manner so obvious that he was hoping for some male camaraderie in this otherwise female domain.

"He's home in bed. Maybe after a slice of banana bread you can go there and get him. No need for you to be underfoot here. I'll keep Regina occupied while we wait for word from Aaron." Aaron, Sarah and Regina discussed who would be in the delivery room with them. Sarah's parents live in Colorado and will be flying in to stay for a month. They won't be here until next week. Sarah and her Mom aren't very close. Sarah knew the Posse would be here to mother her, so she thought them coming after the birth was a good idea. They offered Regina the option to join them in the delivery room of she wanted to. She debated it a long time and finally decided it was best to let them have this private time. She was kicking herself now for that decision. She wishes she were in there or that she had some idea what was going on in there.

The rest of the Posse has arrived. When Lauren waddled in, the nurses came rushing over thinking she was in labor, not a visitor. It was a funny watching them all figure out what was going on. Everyone is sitting around enjoying the coffee and breads and waiting for news.

The first hour rushed by as we all reminisced about the births of our children and my grandchildren. By now, the morning shows were over on the little television and Regina was getting nervous. Last time Aaron was out here, he said Sarah was eight centimeters dilated. That was about half an hour ago. We need to come up with some way to distract Regina so she stops worrying.

There's a commotion out by the nurses' station and when we look up, we see the men come in. Funny how they can never enter a room quietly. When Joe got to my house to get Frankie, they decided to head over to Susan's to get Todd and Bob. On the way up to the maternity ward, they ran into Shamus. The five of them come in like a force to be reckoned with. Regina tries hard to shush them, reminding them they are in a hospital, but it doesn't help. In the commotion, another door opens and Aaron walks out.

"Mom, you have a grandson!" All at once the room goes silent, then Regina lets out a sob and the ruckus begins again. Congratulations are called from all around the room as Aaron walks Regina in to meet her grandson.

ಎ౾

Bob has done an amazing job transforming the open space Aimee leased into a workable facility for her program. She hired a temporary receptionist from the Alliance House to answer phones and hopefully sign up clients. Between the advertising she did and being listed by the insurance companies that accept her, the first four classes filled up. Classes begin in two weeks. Aimee thought this would be a perfect time to visit Michael and his family in Washington DC for a while before jumping into this new venture full force.

Aimee arrived in DC and was greeted with her grandchildren jumping up and down both wanting her full attention. She was struck by how lucky Regina was to be joining the ranks of grandmother and envious that due to the geographical distance, she would never be as close to her grandchildren as she wanted to be. Aimee has never lived close to Michael and his family. Growing up, she and Michael were very close. Since he moved out, they still talk at least once a week, but they've never lived close again. She got over that a long time ago, but every time she sees her grandchildren, she is saddened by it.

Enough with the melancholy. Aimee decided to relax and enjoy this week together with her son's family! Regardless of the weather, Aimee always takes the kids to the zoo. She loves the zoo and has discovered that if you pay attention, you can see the animals all behave in different manners depending on the weather. They have been keeping a log. They know how the lions behave in high humidity verses dry cold, or rain. Same for all the other animals. The kids love going, even now that they are perched on the cusp of their teen years. Aimee will be taking the kids tomorrow and so Michael and Emma can have the day to themselves. It was a tradition the whole family loved.

By week's end, Aimee was exhausted and ready to sleep in her own bed. She would open the Wellness clinic in three days. As Michael drove her to the airport, they talked about the stress Aimee would be putting herself under.

"Mom, I'm worried you are driving yourself too hard. Why couldn't you be happy working at the hospital? Why did you have to take this enormous risk that will make you work so hard?"

Aimee looked at her son and smiled. He was so much like her but couldn't see it. If someone told him to slow down, what would he say? Regardless, she understood where he was coming from. To him, she is old. She should be thinking about retirement, but she isn't ready to pack it in. This is the culmination of her dream. She couldn't pass up the opportunity. Deep down in his heart, Michael knew it. "I'll be fine, Michael. I really want this. I won't let it drive me too hard." They both knew she was kidding herself.

She was off the plane and back home before she knew it. Rather than head straight home, she went to the Wellness clinic to review the final details. Her dream was becoming her reality. All the hard work and sacrifice she went through is paying off right now, today.

The bells on the door jingled and she looked up with misty eyes. There was the Posse. Her Posse. With champagne in hand, we were all there to celebrate this milestone with her.

࿆

Frankie and I had been looking at houses in the San Diego area ever since he got the offer from UCLA. We had been there three or four times on vacation and love it. We always dreamed of retiring there, but never anticipated we'd start with semi-retirement. The houses we looked at are all single story, which is exactly what we want. We are looking for a three bedroom house, with three bathrooms. Ideally, the master suite would be luxurious while the rest to the house would be mainstream. We don't want a mansion to have to maintain, but we want our space to have luxury and pampering built in.

We are grateful for the internet. We are able to search through hundreds of listing and eliminate most of them without even seeing the property. If we think we might like it, we call our agent to visit the property and conduct a walk through using a digital video camera that we can view while she's there. She can show us anything we want to see, from the master bathroom to the view out the living room windows. After further weeding this way, we had a list of five properties to see. We planned a quick trip out to try to narrow it down. If anything else came on the market while we were there, we'd schedule a quick visit.

We left Boston on an early morning flight so we could get a whole day in once we arrived. Our realtor met us at the airport and we were off to the first house. We would be seeing three houses today and two tomorrow. We are staying four days, so we'll have time for second visits and offers if necessary, and I hope it's necessary. I want a house to live in. I'm ready!

The first house was nice, but there were a lot of little things we didn't like. Things that would drive us crazy until we changed them. Like gold fixtures in the bathrooms and different colors for the molding and the window trims. Little things that would require Frankie and I to spend time working inside the house. The second house was perfect except the yard. There really wasn't a private place to put a hot tub. There is no way Frankie or I would agree to a house without a hot tub. On the way to the third house, our realtor got a call about a house that just came on the market. It was on the way to the third house, so we stopped there first.

Perfect! Absolutely perfect! The front yard had lovely landscaping with beautiful flowers in purples, blues and yellows. Frankie chuckled when he saw the blue flowers, remembering our inside joke that he doesn't believe blue exists in nature. The front entry way has a bench next to it with a basket of flowers in it. Once inside the front door, it only gets better.

The living room was designed for entertaining, with a fireplace gracing one wall and a built in liquor station complete with a sink opposite it. I don't see a television in the room, which thrills me and panics Frankie. Much to Frankie's relief, the realtor points out another built cabinet with closing doors hiding a 48 inch flat screen TV. The kitchen looks like something straight out of the Food Network Channel, lots of bright colored appliances and accents on a white background. The layout of the kitchen with its big island is ideal for entertaining. There's a mud room with laundry off the kitchen and a half bath too. Both the kitchen and living room opened onto a deck that has a perfect nook for a hot tub.

Off to the right is the master suite. Off to the left are the guest rooms. We decide to leave the best for last and go left. Two good-sized guest rooms with pleasant views of the yard out the windows. They share a bathroom between the two rooms, complete with a linen closet opening into the hall and into the bathroom. So far, we both love it. Frankie grabs my hand and gives it a squeeze as we walk back through the living room to the master suite.

We open the door to a hallway. That increases the sense of privacy which is important when you know you'll be having lots of overnight guests. They must have put the closets against this wall to create the hallway entry. When we entered the bedroom, our eyes were drawn directly to the sky lights, ceiling fan and vaulted ceiling. Very stately. The room is large, with a king size bed and a reading area with an overstuffed love seat and table. There are two huge closets, mine and his-n-half-mine! The bathroom is amazing! There is a double sink with plenty of counter space. The shower is a two person stall with an over head rain set up and jets along both end walls. The tub is deeper than any I've seen and could easily fit two adults.

This is our house. We canceled the other viewings and make an immediate offer. The asking price was reasonable so that's what we offered. We were able to sign the purchase and sale that day and lined up an inspector for the next day. We walked through the house with the inspector and were thrilled he didn't find anything drastically wrong with the house.

While we were visiting one last time before heading back East, we took video of the house to show the Posse. They would be happy for us, and happy they have rooms available whenever they visit.

On the flight home, I snuggled against Frankie's shoulder. "I can't believe we are moving away from Massachusetts. I never thought I would."

He kisses my head and reassures me, "Juliette, California isn't as far away as it used to be. Look, we were there and back in five days. With a direct flight, it's a piece of cake. Don't worry about it. The Posse won't fall apart. You'll visit them and they'll visit you. Don't be sad."

He always knew what to say. Content with our trip and soothed by his words, I fell asleep against his chest.

გოჯ

Susan came in looking like she had a grudge with the world. "Susan, what's wrong?" I asked before turning on the teapot.

"I slept with Bob".

Oh my God. No preamble, no 'sit down, I have something to tell you'. Just 'I slept with Bob'. How do I react to that? "Susan, sit down. Tell me what happened."

"Todd went to Boy Scout camp this weekend. He has his heart set on becoming an Eagle Scout and spends every opportunity he can earning badges. This weekend, the Cub Scouts were going camping and they needed help. He could earn a Leadership badge by working with the counselors and helping the Cubs."

"What does this have to do with sleeping with Bob? Get to it already." The teapot was screaming so I got us both tea and Susan continued.

"I took Todd to the bus where he met the other scouts. He quickly got into his 'I'm in charge' mode and shooed me away. On my drive home, I decided to get take out and a movie. I called Bob to see if he'd be around and if he wanted to join me. We decided I'd get the food and he'd get a movie. I got Thai food and a nice bottle of wine. We settled down in front of the TV to watch the movie while we ate."

I was starting to think this could take forever to get to what happened. I also knew that if I tried to push her along, she would clam up and not tell me anything. I had nowhere to go. I decided to let her unwind the story as slowly as she wanted to.

"We ate slowly, picking from the cartons long after we declared we were full. The movie turned out to be one of those 'friend turned lover' stories. The guy helps the woman try to make it work with her loser boyfriend and when he breaks her heart, she turns to the friend, and then they kiss. It was so predictable and when the movie ended, I turned to Bob. He was looking at me in an odd way. I looked at him questioningly, and he reached out to touch my cheek. I closed my eyes at his touch. When I opened them, he was still right there. I leaned forward and kissed him. I don't know why. I have no idea what came over me, but I kissed him, and he kissed me back."

Okay, I needed Susan to take a breath. Neither one of us had touched our tea and it was cold. "Stop there for a minute. Let me get us some hot tea. I'll be right back."

Susan took a few steadying breaths while I put the tea pot back on. This is crazy! What can possibly come of this? Bob is young enough to be… Well, he has to be fifteen years younger than Susan.

"Okay, I'm back. Keep going."

Susan took a quick sip of her hot tea. "Thanks for the tea. Where was I? So I kissed him and he kissed me back. When I pulled away, I said 'Bob, I'm sorry. I didn't mean' and he cut me off. He said 'I'm glad you kissed me. I wanted to kiss you but I was too afraid.' So we kissed again. I was so glad Todd wasn't there and wouldn't be home all weekend. After a while, I asked him if he wanted to go upstairs. He asked if I meant together. I said I did. What was I thinking? Is this crazy?"

How do I answer that? "No, I don't think it's crazy. Unexpected, certainly, but not crazy. You are a beautiful woman and he's a hunk. You are living under the same roof, co-parenting a teenage son. You share all the responsibilities a couple share. It's not completely unexpected you'd share, well, everything a couple does."

She sighed. Susan doesn't fall for a guy often, but when she does, she falls hard. I worry about how this might impact Todd. "Do you think this was a one-time thing or do you think it will keep happening?"

"It's already been more than a one-time thing. We slept together all weekend, and had a wonderful time I might add. We decided we'd do our own thing for a couple hours then meet for dinner somewhere to discuss what we do now. If this is going to be something we try for real, we need to decide what we'll tell Todd. Things are complicated because if we try and it doesn't work, Todd loses and that's not fair."

"Yes, but if you try and it works, you all win."

"That's why it's so hard."

❧

The next afternoon I got a call from Shamus. When the twins were little, I'd worry every time my phone displayed Shamus' number. I finally figured out he was probably calling for a baby sitter and not to tell me some dire story about an accident. I answered this call as casually as all recent calls.

"Lauren's in labor and we are on the way to the hospital."

Unbelievable! A baby is being born in the middle of the afternoon? That never happens. "We'll be there right away" I assure Shamus and hang up.

The Posse arrives about half an hour after Lauren and Shamus. She is already fully dilated and ready to push. Frankie and Joe want to start a pool and can't decide whether to base the pool on delivery time, weight or gender of the baby. They debate a minute too long and Shamus bursts into the waiting room.

"We have our girl! Paige Margaret, and she's perfect!"

We give Lauren a few minutes to rest and then all rush in. We have flowers, stuffed animals and all Lauren's favorite foods. She looks good, relaxed. She certainly doesn't look like she just had a baby. Like her mother, Paige is gorgeous. She has blond curls, nothing like the twins who were baldies until well past their first birthdays.

"I am so excited to have a girl!" Lauren gushes. "Is that disrespectful of the twins?"

"Of course not" we all assure her. "You've had your boys. Now it's time for a daughter. Finally you get to dress a baby in all the ruffles and bows you want. I just hope she doesn't become a tom boy before you get your fill of playing dress up."

We pass Paige around and take turns cooing. I know Frankie and I will be stopping on the way home to buy lots of little dresses and pink outfits. He has always loved buying baby gifts, and I love that soft side of him.

After about an hour, we decide to leave Lauren and Shamus to celebrate together. I remember the night the twins were born and how afraid they were. Two little babies both needing them was an overwhelming responsibility. The twins are amazing adults now, thanks to the parenting job they did. Lauren and Shamus made parenting their number one responsibility and it paid off. It was a huge change from the life they lead before. They are about to embark on another adventure late in life, and they couldn't look happier.

Chapter 12
The Long Road Home

I officially handed over the keys to Alliance House today. The programs I began there so long ago are fully implemented and running successfully. Alliance House has become a premiere center of excellence for other shelters to use as their model to create similar programs. I'm very proud that I made a difference. I worked in high tech collecting a huge salary for twenty five years. None of that compares to the feeling of accomplishment I got from the volunteer work I did at Alliance House. I may not have earned a salary, but the look on the face of those women as they aced an interview, started a new job, and got their own place to live in safety trumped any paycheck, hands down.

Frankie and I signed papers selling the house yesterday. Even if we weren't moving to San Diego, we'd be selling the house. We have so many happy memories there from raising the kids, but it is too big. We don't need all that space any more. The house we found in San Diego is perfect for us. Big enough to encourage lots of visitors, but not big enough to allow children, or grandchildren for that matter, to move in.

Tonight the Posse is taking Lauren out. It will be her first time leaving Paige alone with Shamus. I'm not sure who's more nervous about that, Lauren or Shamus. Shamus was a great dad to the twins and had no problem being alone with them for hours at a time, even when they were newborns. That was a long, long time ago.

I picked Lauren up and we headed over to Aimee's. She decided it had been so long since she cooked for us, that tonight was a perfect night to make up for that. Tonight is the night I'm going to tell the Posse when I'm leaving.

Dinner was delicious as always. Lauren tried to convince Aimee to cook for her all the time. "I need to get rid of this baby weight. I thought it was tough when I was 25. I'm sure it's going to be much harder at 46!" We all laughed. I wondered how long you could get away calling it baby fat. My babies are all adults now. I guess it's too late for me.

Over dessert, I decide it's time. "Well, my time here is drawing to a close." All eyes were on me, and they were disbelieving eyes. "Come on guys, you knew this was coming. Frankie and I closed on the house. I wrapped up my work at Alliance House. Frankie finishes up next week. We have our trek mapped out, and we are almost ready to go."

The looks reflected back at me were so sad. I felt like I was killing someone's puppy. This was such a hard decision and I really need the Posse's support. I start feeling bad, like I'm making a huge mistake. "Please, don't make me feel bad."

Regina was the first one to smile, "Jules, I'm so happy for you. I know we'll still see each other. You are only a plane ride away, and you are in a place that's warm in the winter. You won't be able to get rid of us!" I relaxed a little bit hearing her support. She looked at the others and glared a bit. "We all support you and understand what you are doing. This is a great opportunity for Frankie and sets you both up for retirement. We are all happy for you, right girls?" Again she looked around.

Aimee looked dejected. "I appreciate all the help you gave me getting the Wellness Clinic up and running. I know I couldn't have done it without you. I am thrilled you are starting a business helping others start businesses, and I'm honored to have been amongst your first clients. It wouldn't be so bad if you were staying here and helping women locally, but you are going clear across the country. I'm afraid you are going to replace us."

"Oh Aimee, that will never happen. How could I ever find a group like you? You can't get rid of me just because I'm leaving town."

At that, the mood lightened considerably and we all chatted while enjoying our coffee and dessert. I'm sure they'll all get closer when I leave. I will have to work hardest to be sure I don't fall out of the fold.

Over coffee, Lauren let me know her decision, "I decided I won't be staying home with Paige. I'm going back to work." I knew this was weighing heavy on her heart and mind and I was glad they had made a decision.

"What made you decide?"

"Shamus and I talked a lot about it. With the twins, we had twice the amount to do all the time. Two doctor's appointments, two haircuts, two of everything."

"I know. I remember how crazy it was when I babysat. Mine were far enough apart in age that Marie could help out with Jason. With the twins, it was four years before they could reliably get their own coats on and with the twins you went back to work."

"Yeah, but I worked at home two days a week. I'd drop the boys off, and then go home. I didn't have to worry about dressing up and I could do laundry while I was working. It was ideal."

"But with Paige…"

"Right. With Paige, I don't think it will be as hard because it's just one baby and two of us. Though Shamus said something the other night that pissed me off, then I realized he was probably right. He said with the twin we were much younger, I was much younger. I had all the energy in the world to chase after those two. I've slowed down a lot. I'm not twenty five any more. My back and knees creak when I get up and down from the floor. "

"Ouch! That must have hurt to hear, but I think he's right. No one likes to hear they aren't getting any younger, but I'd rather accept that painful message than discover the truth of it a few week after quitting a job I love."

"I know. I was so mad at him I wouldn't talk to him. When I realized he was right, I decided to cook a fancy dinner for him. Paige was fussy that day. By the time I had her settled, I ended up ordering pizza and looking up daycare centers on line."

That is so like Lauren. Always prepared with a 'Plan B' in case something happens to deflate her lofty ideas. After coffee we are going to look at daycare centers. The one the twins went to is still there and we'll visit that one first.

"Have you talked to your boss since Paige was born?"

"Yes, I went in to work late last week to introduce Paige around. Of course everyone loved her! I got a few more presents. I love that people are thoughtful, but I look at each gift box as another thank you note I have to write. I asked about working part time, but I guess that won't work. He did agree to let me work from home two days a week."

"Just like the old days" I say and we both smile. It is just like the old days.

There is one more week until Frankie and I leave. The girls decided they would host dinners in my honor in their homes. Some invited the men of the Posse, others didn't. Tonight was Susan's turn and it was just the Posse. No men. Bob took Todd out for pizza with Frankie and Joe. Then they were going to bring a pizza to Shamus who was home with Paige.

Susan looked really happy. "I know I should be sad because you are leaving, Jules, but I can't help it. I'm so happy!"

"Susan, I don't want anyone to be sad that I'm leaving. Me being gone won't change anything! Tell us all about that glow."

Susan smiled, and when she smiles she simply glows. I am so used to seeing her serious about her job, that seeing her truly happy is still a surprise after all these years. "It's Bob. Since I slept with him, he's been wonderful."

The shock on Aimee, Regina and Lauren's faces is priceless. Obviously Susan had only shared her secret with me. Lauren recovers first. "What? When? How come..." Okay, maybe this isn't recovering first, it sounds like Lauren is blabbering.

Susan giggled, yes, giggled. "A few weeks ago when Todd went to Boy Scout camp, it just happened."

Aimee was there with "that doesn't 'just happen'. Not with you, Susan!"

"You're right. Bob has been great with Todd. He is such a good role model, with his school and work ethic. I couldn't ask for a better example. The work he did on the Wellness Clinic for Aimee is impressive. I was thrilled when he let Todd come and help on the weekends. Todd learned a lot from him. Bob is completely different than the men Todd's mother lived with after he was born. I think Bob loves Todd like a son, even without a paternity test to prove it."

"Enough about Bob and Todd. We all know he's a great dad. Tell us about what kind of man he is. What kind of lover!" Regina was never one to let a good love story linger untold, especially when it involved smut!

"The weekend Todd went to camp, Bob and I got take out and a movie. He picked the movie and I picked the food."

"South East Asia?" Aimee asked? She and Regina couldn't be less alike in the arena of love stories.

"It doesn't matter what they ate!" Regina retorted.

Susan laughed at their predictability and continued her story. "I kissed him first. He touched my face with such a gentle hand I melted. I bent in and kissed him. When he kissed me back, I was so relieved. I was really afraid I might have ruined everything. We spent that weekend getting to know each other intimately. We already knew each other so well as friends, roommates and co-parents. Exploring each other's bodies was like when the lights come back on after a power outage. You are surprised by what you find right in front of you. We found each other."

I couldn't help but wonder who would ask the question on all of our minds. I guess I'll do it. That way, if Susan gets mad at me, I won't be around long and she'll forget she's mad by the time we see each other again. "He is really young...." I left my voice trail off making a question out of the statement. No need to point out that my children are older than he is.

"Yes, he is young. I guess putting it that way is better than saying I'm old, but what difference does it make? We both love Todd and want to be there to raise him. If we can love each other too, we'll have something left when Todd moves on. Which will be before you know it." She's right. Todd will be leaving for college in a few years and kids seldom really move home after college.

"Susan, you're not doing this because you are afraid to be alone, are you?" I don't remember if it was Aimee or Lauren who asked. It was a good question, and one Susan needed to consider.

"No, I've been alone. I'm good alone. I have adult friends and we do adult things. I love going to museums and visiting artists. I have my sisters, my nieces and nephews. Probably more importantly, I have you guys. I'm not worried about being alone. I think back to how things were before Todd. When all my time was my own. I wasn't lonely then, I was just a little bit sad. Todd took that sadness away. Now Bob, Bob makes me feel like a woman again. What Bob gives me is something I had long ago given up on. If it doesn't last forever, I'm okay with it."

Susan sounds like she's made her decision, a decision that will allow her some well deserved happiness for a change. "So the big question I have for you guys is how do we tell Todd that Bob and I are sleeping together?"

Business has been gradually increasing for Aimee and the Wellness Clinic was featured in the Sunday magazine section of the Boston Globe. Apparently a guy in the executive management at the paper and his wife went to the clinic as clients and were happy with what they learned. He sent a reporter to write a feature article for the paper. Aimee was on the cover with a group of clients in the clinic.

Aimee was glowing when she walked in to brunch with copies of the paper for each of us. I think she is happier now that she's a star in print than she was when she got her financing, or when Bob finished the renovation. "I can't believe how good I sound in this. That reporter should be writing fiction."

It was Susan who retorted Aimee's self-degradation, although we all felt the same way. "Come on Aimee! Look at everything you've done. You have reinvented yourself and created a business that helps people improve their health in a way that insurance companies support and therefore fund. It's a huge win for people trying to get healthy who just don't have the tools to do it on their own."

I am so happy I was here to see Aimee's dream fulfilled. She had worked so hard for it, and deserved the success she was having. I am worried about Aimee working too hard, she did have that tendency in the past. Rather than her typical dismissal of my concerns, Aimee agrees.

With a wink to me, Aimee says "my business advisor stressed two things I had to have in place before starting a business. One is a backup so things can run if I have an emergency or illness. The second is an exit strategy. I listened to her for the first one. As you'd expect, I ignored the second." We all laughed at her because listening to advice isn't her strong suit, and I was happy she listened to any of it.

"Remember the woman I hired from Alliance House? She did such a great job as a receptionist, learning to do things the way I wanted them then gently suggesting alternatives. I was so impressed, I decided to review my class notes with her. Here she made suggestions as well, and I really liked some of them. I asked her to sit through my classes to see how I run them. The next step will be to have her teach them." I am amazed that Aimee is willing to let go of control a little bit.

"Who is answering the phones now?" Regina asked. If her receptionist is going to be teaching classes, that's a great question.

Aimee said proudly "I've hired a second woman from Alliance House. I talked to Jules's replacement in the career program about having a rotating position to help women gain clerical experience. It seems like a natural marriage of efforts enabling people to better themselves."

What Aimee is doing is amazing. She is giving back to the community two-fold. I wish the article written on her could have revealed the opportunity Aimee was giving these women, but Alliance House has strict privacy rules and she wouldn't risk exposing her employee's identities for fear their abusers might find them.

"I think I'll be able to run about ten classes a week with ten people per session. I'd also like to see about fifteen private clients a week. With half that number, we cover expenses and minimal salaries for everyone including me. With the full number, we cover expenses and hire more, allowing me enough time to continue developing programs and keeping the information fresh. We have the space and time slots for double that. If we get double that, I'll have to clone myself! Won't that be a great problem to have!"

֍

Regina and I got together for coffee two days before I was leaving. "I can't believe I won't be able to just stop by any time I want to anymore." Since she and Joe got married, she hasn't been stopping by very much, but I didn't point that out to her.

"How is that gorgeous grandbaby of yours doing?" I ask, trying to divert her from discussing me leaving. I don't want us both crying again.

"I just want to eat him up" she says, and I know she must have squeezed those thighs a million times already. Especially since they are chubby. "Sarah said he's been sleeping through the night since he was about a week old. She feeds him right before he goes to bed and he sleeps six hours. Remember when our kids were little?"

"I remember calling you up saying 'you up?' and you saying 'I am now'. You were such a good friend to keep me company on those long nights."

"You did the same for me a few years later."

"Now it's Aaron's turn. Babies are so much fun, but they are exhausting. When is Sarah going back to work?"

"I don't know why she doesn't stay home. Aaron can support the family. At least for a few years." Regina isn't happy Sarah is going back to work. She would have stayed home to raise Aaron if they could have afforded it, but they needed her income. Regina would never say anything to Aaron or Sarah about her disappointment that Sarah is pursuing her career and not staying home with the baby. She had plenty of second guessers when she was raising Aaron, and unsolicited advice was always something she hated. She hated receiving it so much that she was certainly not going to give it.

"I'm sure they'll work it out. We all did what was right for us at the time. Twenty years later, we still worry whether we made the right choice. Sarah and Aaron will be no different from us in that regard. Now tell me, how is Joe? Is he still Mr. Wonderful?" We both chuckled at the use of the name the Posse gave Joe long before we met him. For weeks, all we ever heard was 'Joe said this. Joe did that" and every comment was accentuated with a starry eyed look.

Regina cringes when she thinks of it, but deep down inside, she still feels the same way. "He's great. We're great. I love being married to him. Joe likes to cook. Can you believe that? Not just fancy, only for the holidays, or only for a party kind of cooking. Joe likes to make steak and salad for dinner, or pasta with meatballs. He makes things that I'll eat and he makes them on weeknights. I would say he's cooked about half the meals since we've been married."

"That's a surprise, and unexpected for sure!"

"At night, we'll hang out the in the kitchen. One of us cooks while the other sorts the mail, sets the table, and maybe empties the dishwasher. It's together time where we are doing the everyday work of living. I have never had that kind of relationship before."

I smile a knowing smile because that's exactly what Frankie and I have always had. We are a team through the work and the play of life. "Regina, I'm so happy for you. I'm so happy you decided to go against your better judgment and buy a Bruins ticket from a scalper." Since that fateful decision, Regina's enjoyed a breathtaking romance and married the man with the golden ticket, the Black and Gold 'season tickets'!

୶୶

Frankie and I decide to host a final going away brunch at The Daily Paper. We've been going there so much that it feels like they're part of the family we're leaving. The Posse all come with their other halves, kids, grandkids, everyone we'll miss once we hit the road.

Frankie knows this will be hard for me, I've never liked saying good-bye. He assures me that this isn't really good bye. This morning before heading to the Paper, he said "we'll be hosting visitors before we are completely unpacked." I'm sure he's right since we'll be arriving in San Diego in time for winter semester at UCLA. I'm certain someone will want to visit San Diego rather than suffer through the non-stop continuum of bleak, cold New England winter weather.

Before long, mimosas are being poured and people start telling stories. How they met me, what they thought of Frankie when I brought him home. Stories buried so deep in memories that I swear half of them are total fiction. We talked about the 'ones that got away' and the 'ones that didn't leave soon enough', and of course the ones we kept. We reminisced about our children's births and then their children's births. Time flew by.

At last, all that was left were the girls, the Posse. Frankie slipped away too, giving us the privacy we needed for our final farewell. "Promise me you'll come visit all the time!"

Of course they'll come. Aimee and Regina even did their standard bickering of who would get to sleep with Susan. Ever since our first 'girls only' vacation, there has been bickering over who gets to sleep with Susan. "It's my house, I get to decide who sleeps with Susan. And if I want to sleep with her, then you two are stuck with each other!" At that, we all start giggling.

"I can't believe I'm leaving you guys. What am I going to do? Am I making a stupid move? I know we always said we'd retire somewhere warm, but I never thought I'd be the first to go. Seriously, promise you won't get so caught up in your own lives that you forget about me." As I say it, tears start rolling down my cheeks.

Lauren tells me that she'll be out to visit with Paige the week Shamus goes to San Francisco on business. "I figured I'd leave when he does, then he can fly down to meet us. Will you have a crib or should I bring Paige's pack and play?"

"We'll be there over Valentine's week" Regina assures me. "Joe and Frankie have to cook for us like they did last year."

I chuckled at the memory. "Good thing you aren't leaving Frankie on his own to cook for me. As impressive as Joe is in the kitchen, Frankie is not. He makes a fine sous-chef to Joe, but an Iron Chef he will never be. Unless you happen to be craving a ham and salami sandwich!"

Aimee plans to be out in the summer. She expects there to be a slow down at the Wellness clinic then, so it would be the right time to hand over the reins to see how the team does. "They'll have been working with me for almost a year by then. I'm sure they will do well on their own." This career change has done wonders for slowing Aimee down and making her give up control a little bit. The old Aimee never would have left her business in someone else's hands for a week. This Aimee has been grooming a team to do just that.

Susan isn't sure when she'll make it out to visit or who she'll bring. She and Bob told Todd they were dating and Todd was full of questions and concerns. "Todd asked me if Bob and I break up, who gets to keep him. The poor kid is so afraid of losing people he loves. I understand it, but his life has been more stable in the past three years than it ever was. He has me, my parents, siblings and nieces and nephews, and he has you guys. For the past year, he's had Bob. I know he loves us all, I just can't seem to convince him that I'm not going anywhere."

Regina went through some of this with Aaron when she got divorced. "Kids don't understand the world doesn't revolve around them. They see themselves as the star and everything happens to them. More often than not, they are just a pawn being used in someone else's game or not even thought about at all. It's sad when they finally realize the truth. That's the first step in understanding the terms of their relationships with people and to take some ownership over the relationship. It's hard, but it's all part of growing up."

Susan gave Regina a hug. "Thank you! You always have the right words to say. Hey, if I go out to visit over Valentines week, you could sleep with me instead of Joe!" That was exactly what we needed to get this party back on a happy note.

I wasn't going to let Susan get away without a commitment on visiting. "Susan, I think you should come out to visit alone. Let Bob and Todd bond without you. Bob needs to understand what being a father is really like. Since you've never had any complaints, I'd guess he has the role of lover/husband down just fine." Susan agreed to both a visit and that Bob does just fine in that department.

༺༻

At last it's time to go. Frankie and I decided to take our time driving across country, visiting everything we wanted to see on the east coast before meandering toward our new home. The moving truck is gone and our belongings will be put away in storage for a few months. By then, we'll be in our new home, ready to unpack.

I'm a little less nervous now that I've seen the Posse. I brought them together all those years ago, and they have forged friendships with each other that will continue to grow without me here. I will stay close to each of them, and we'll get together as often as possible on both coasts throughout the years. I'm confident we'll stay together. The Posse is too strong to let distance break it up. I feel tears start rolling down my cheeks again...

Our trip to the west coast will be reminiscent of a trip I made to Louisiana when I was in college. We visited 22 states in two weeks. Massachusetts to Louisiana and back via Chicago? I guess that is the only justification for Sanibel Island, Florida being en route from Massachusetts to San Diego.

Frankie and I make our first stop to bid farewell to New York City and Broadway. We'll have dinner before the show then leave in the morning. The only choice for dinner is corned beef sandwiches from Katz. Over dinner, we talk about when we might be in the city next. We've been going to the city almost once a month for some reason or another. Not anymore. We decide the sandwiches are so good, we should get a couple to toss in to the cooler for lunch tomorrow. We see the classic My Fair Lady, which neither of us had seen on Broadway before. It was fantastic.

We meander south, stopping at Graceland and Opryland, our tributes to singers we admire. Over lunch, we sympathize with the tragedy that sometimes follows talented stars so closely on the heels of their success. We wonder at the strength some people possess to keep tragedy at bay. "I worry about the young stars of today, people like Taylor Swift and Justin Bieber. Will they be able to keep the demons of success from corrupting them?"

Frankie takes my hand "Sweetheart, let's worry about our kids and grandbabies. Let's not borrow problems from the stars." As usual, he's right. I have a tendency to borrow problems from other people and miss the magic I have right here in my little world. Luckily Frankie's around to keep me grounded.

We are spending a week on Sanibel Island. I have always wanted to go there, ever since I heard about the shells you find strolling the beaches. We arrive in mid October, so there are no crowds. The front porch of the B&B we are renting opens right on the water. We take long walks during the day, eating at whatever shanty we find that smells good when hunger strikes. In the evening, we share a bottle of wine on the beach and watch the sun dip low over the water. Sunsets are the perfect ingredient for romance, and Frankie doesn't let me down. Our nights bring on renewed passion, fueled by love and adventure, with a little sprinkling of anxiety of what we'll find in this next phase of our lives.

In what seems like a flash, our week is over and it's time to move on. There aren't many stops planned between here and the Grand Canyon. Just lots of open road and a GPS that's great at pointing out nearby attractions. We want to be settled into our new home by Thanksgiving, so we have roughly four weeks to get 3000 miles. Piece of cake!

༺༻

We spent each day driving in a westerly direction. After about 250 miles, we start discussing where we would like to stay. We cruise the Internet looking for interesting sites within a 100 mile radius and find a place to sleep nearby. We generally stay two nights in each location. That gives us an entire day to explore, then after a good night sleep, we start out fresh the next morning.

We stopped in Vicksburg Mississippi to visit the National Military Park there. I never realized the Civil War battles pushed so far south. Frankie laughs at my geographical and historical naivety. Give me a good love story and I'll remember every detail, maybe even make up a few of my own, but I can't remember anything about the history I learned in school. Nor would I be surprised if you told me North Virginia and New Mexico share a border.

Frankie had been looking forward to our stop in Kansas. We are going to go in search of the best steak in Kansas. We've been avoiding red meat for a week so we'll be craving it! We decide we would ask locals for recommendations. We'll try four recommended places and pick our favorite. The thing about Frankie is he is limited in his taste in food. He could eat a New York strip steak every night for a month, and never tire of it. Of course I'll mull over the menu and select something different every night. Unless my cravings for ribs kicks in, in which case I'll be as boring as Frankie in my selections!

We are not disappointed. We easily get four recommendations to try out and after four delicious meals, we both agree to a winner. It is a local dive run by a husband and wife called Beef. When we arrived, we were surprised at the menu. "Do you have any chicken?" I asked. The owner looked at me, pointed to the sign over the bar and laughed a big belly laugh. The sign, of course read 'Beef'. I guess I won't be getting any chicken tonight. Hands down, this was the best place. We decided we'd go back for lunch on our way out of town. Yummy. We'll miss this place.

It's early November and there is already snow in some of the higher elevations along our way. We planned to stop in Denver for a week to visit some old friends, but decide to cut the visit short and only stay two nights. It's nice to stay in someone's home rather than another hotel and enjoy some home cooked meals. I don't miss the food shopping or doing the dishes after eating. I do miss Frankie making me an omelet cooked perfectly or seeing his smile when I give him scallops sautéed with just the right amount of garlic. There are two sets of friends we know in Denver that we worked with in the past. They didn't know each other before our visit, but it was obvious they would become fast friends. On our final night in Denver, Frankie and I cooked dinner for the six of us and we shared a late night of stories and laughs.

We are making two more stops before getting home, and you can tell we are both getting tired of living out of suitcases. Ever since we brought the children and grandchildren to the Grand Canyon, I've wanted to come back. Our last time was so hectic, we got caught up in every tourist trap. I wanted to see it again in peace, at my own pace. At last, here we are, overlooking the most amazing vision I've ever seen. Frankie squeezes my hand and murmurs how small the canyon makes him feel. It defines the word awesome. We snap some pictures, though we already know they'll never do it justice.

"I want to come back. I want to go down there and look up." I'm shocked as I hear myself say this. I'm the one who hates bugs and won't camp. If I have to ride a mule I will. Somehow I want to get to the bottom and look up. I want to see the majesty from the view of the stream that created the wonder.

As we leave the Grand Canyon, Frankie pulls over at the Hoover Dam. This wasn't a planned stop, but I knew he'd want to visit. This is the kind of engineering feat that fascinates Frankie. I love seeing the respect shine in his eyes for the creators of the engineering marvel. We stay a few hours and after completing the tour, head for the lights of Las Vegas.

ঔ৽

Again, we planned to stay five nights, but just want to be home. After checking into the Trump Hotel, I call the storage company to arrange for our belongings to be delivered in three days. We are about five and a half hours from our new home. We'll get there the day before our stuff and have just enough time to decide where we want everything. I'm so glad our realtor suggested having a cleaning agency prepare the house for our move in. That's one less thing we'll have to do.

For the next two nights, we'll behave like newlyweds, living it up in Las Vegas! Regina taught me Black Jack on one of our 'girls only' cruises many years ago. Frankie enjoys watching me play my conservative hands, winning a little at a time until I cash out and surprise the dealer and everyone at the table with the pile of chips I walk away with. From there, we head to the poker table where Frankie plays and I watch. I find it hard not asking questions about his cards, so I wander off to a slot machine nearby.

"Are you having a good time?"

"Yes, I am. I had to leave you because I was afraid I was going to say something about your hand and get in trouble." As I finished a pull on the one armed bandit, I looked up. Instead of seeing Frankie there, it was Donald. The Donald. Donald Trump! I couldn't believe my eyes.

"Hello Mr. Trump. I... I..."

"I was just over at the poker table. Your husband told me you are a fan of mine, so I thought I'd come over and say hello."

Somehow, a calm came over me and I got back on my professional footing. "Mr. Trump, could we get a cup of coffee? I'd love the opportunity to talk with you."

"Call me Donald. I like a person who would offer me coffee in my own house, when the liquor is flowing freely. Sure, let's go find a quiet corner and talk."

He led me off to a conference room that could have been command central, full of monitors, headsets and recording equipment. "Your husband told me you spent your entire career hoping to work for a good boss. You've never had one?"

"No, I've worked over twenty five years in high tech and never had a good boss. That's not to say I didn't learn from each of them, I did. From many of them, I learned traits I never want to have. From fewer of them, I learned positive traits for leading people or running a business. Unfortunately every one of them was pursuing their own agenda without regard for the people in their paths and I can't respect advancement at the expense of your peers and subordinates. I have watched your career and the Apprentice for years and I don't see that in you. I'm not blind, I know you aren't a nurturer and that you call it like you see it. I respect that. I don't want to be coddled, but I don't want to be a pawn either. From what I understand, you don't do either of those."

Donald smiled. "You sound a little bit like a Girl Scout."

"I was and I'm a mother. That being said, I think baking cookies for your coworkers is a nice thing to do. They remember those cookies when they have to work all night to finish a project I need to present to the board the next day. I can count on them. In return, they are loyal to me for respecting them."

After so many years of dreaming it, Donald asked me the question I've been waiting to hear "would you consider working for me? You don't have to work in real estate. I could use someone like you in human resources, motivating middle management in leadership techniques." How I would have jumped at those words two years ago.

"I'm sorry Donald, I'm working with abused women now. I started a program in Boston that helped women in a safe shelter get their lives back by learning a marketable skill, then securing a job that could sustain them and their children. The program has been a grand success and I'm going to start a second one at a shelter in San Diego. For me it's no longer about the paycheck. It's about giving back to society. What I would like from you, if possible Donald, would be a willingness to hire some clients for clerical positions within your firms?"

I can't believe, after dreaming for so long I am turning Donald Trump down. We hear a knock on the door and see Frankie there with a gorgeous young woman. "Mr. Trump, this gentleman is here to collect his wife."

"Thank you for the opportunity Donald" I said as we shook hands.

"Here's my card with my direct line. Let me know when you are set up and can begin providing me clerical help." Frankie's jaw drops. He never expected I'd get a private meeting, and certainly never anticipated I'd get help from Donald at the clinic.

Taking Freddie's hand, I said "come on sweetheart", "let's go home. Good night Donald and thank you."

We left the conference room, found our car and drove home to San Diego. The last leg of our trip is over. We are home.

Chapter 13
One Year Later

I am so excited to be heading back East to visit the Posse and our family. "I can't believe we've been gone a year already." Frankie and I are on a red eye landing at 7:30 in the morning in Boston.

Frankie grunts a little as he says "it doesn't seem like a year because we've had so much company. We knew to expect a lot, but I don't think we went longer than three weeks without someone visiting. I'm glad the kids got out here for a visit and I'm glad they were comfortable leaving the grandkids longer and letting them fly home alone." I smiled at him.

"What?" Frankie asks.

"You always said we'd never babysit the grandkids for a week while their parents went on vacation but we had both sets of grandkids for two week!" Frankie laughed and gave me his 'you're right' look. I grab a blanket and pillow and settle in. I really want to get some sleep on the flight. I don't want to waste any time during our visit sleeping!

In what seemed like no time, Frankie was nudging my shoulder. "Come on, I want to sleep." I say as I try to push away in the seat.

"We're landing."

Suddenly I'm wide awake. I can't wait to see the Posse! We are gathering for an afternoon visit and dinner at Aimee's house while Frankie hangs out with guys. We are both looking forward to catching up with everyone.

※

When I get to Aimee's, the Posse is already there. I was never the last one to arrive. I guess some things have changed in the past year. We all start talking at once. "Wait, wait, I can't hear any of you. We need to take turns. Susan, you go first."

Susan is bursting and I know she won't be able to listen if she doesn't spill first. "We had the paternity test done, Bob is Todd's father. " Susan was so uncertain about proving paternity, either way, that I wonder what changed her mind. "Todd is taking biology in high school. He did his blood typing and found out his blood is B Negative. He also learned about gene traits and dominance and all that. He kept saying 'my mom had blue eyes and if my dad had...'. He'd look at Bob with that question in his eyes. I asked them if they wanted to have the test done. They both said they did."

"What if the results prove that Bob isn't his father?"

"We talked about that a lot. If Bob isn't Todd's biological father, we were going to see if Bob could adopt him. That would give Bob and Todd a legal connection should anything ever happen to me. If Bob is Todd's biological father, we just had to have Todd's birth certificate updated and Bob's name added."

This was great news. The curiosity was killing me, "so you are one big happy family?"

"Yup, we are."

"What does that mean?"

"Bob and I are happily living together as lovers, and parents to Todd. We're a really happy little family. We even have movie night where Todd cooks dinner for us and Bob and I clean up after the movie. Being a mother is so much different when there's a father in the picture to depend on! Being a single mom was fine, but sharing the joys and the worries of parenthood with someone spreads the burden but multiplies the joy. I don't understand it.. You guys are great, and I love sharing with you, but you don't keep the bed warm at night, if you know what I mean!"

We all toast to that, although Aimee and Regina put on a little show of annoyance that Susan would pick Bob over them as bed mates. Susan's life has changed so much in the past few years. She has a new perspective and balance in her life. She seems truly happy for the first time in a long time.

I tell everyone about my new center. "It's very similar to Alliance House and I've managed to build up a network of companies willing to give women a fresh start. It's hard starting from scratch, but I feel good about the progress. Frankie's only working part time, which is great. We're making the most of being retired part-time." I finish with a big smile for each of them, "we've also been busy with all the company we've had." They've all visited and love the new house. I even have a drawer allocated for each of them, so they can just show up and not worry about packing a bag.

Regina is pulling out pictures of Aaron and Sarah's baby to share, so we let her go next. The baby is 18 months old. He is running around non-stop and filling a hole in Regina's heart that she held special for a grandchild to occupy.

"How are the newlyweds? Are you still called newlyweds?" I ask.

"Joe makes me so happy. I swear I will never cook again! He loves to cook! He rubs my neck while I'm doing the dishes, which is why the dishes usually end up staying in the sink until morning." Regina has always been a sucker for a backrub and I can't blame Joe for finding this button and exploiting it to get what he wants, especially when what he wants is obviously satisfying Regina!

Susan jumped in to add "Joe and Bob have become good friends and the four of us spend a lot of time together. I like that Todd has other happy couples around him. It's good for him to see that there are good people in the world."

Susan is beaming with motherly joy as she describes the latest arrangement. "Joe discovered that Todd likes to babysit and we set him up with Aaron and Sarah. It's a win-win because they felt guilty leaving him with me to go out on dates. Todd gets to earn some pocket money, and Joe, Susan, Bob and I can go out for our own date night."

I'm beginning to feel a little bit jealous that they are getting along just fine without me. They are even forging deeper relationships with each other, filling the hole I left when Frankie and I moved out west. Lauren can tell I'm getting sad and gets right to the heart of it.

"I miss you so much, Jules, and Paige misses her Auntie! The twins tell her all about Auntie Green Beans and stories about how you were like their fairy godmother. You were, you know? Paige is ready to stake her claim on her Auntie Green Beans!" I feel a little better. Lauren fills us in on the twins' college progress and Shamus's work.

"I'm still working from home two days a week, although on those two days, I'm doing less work and more errands. I am putting in a solid forty hours a week, but that's all. I'm too old to keep up the pace I did before." Too old, what is she talking about? Lauren is the baby of our group. If she's too old to keep up the pace, what about the rest of us?

Aimee is finally done fussing around the kitchen and sits down with us. "The Wellness Clinic is doing amazingly well. We are profitable and I've hired a second dietician and have six part time workers from Alliance House. I am thinking about expanding to a second location."

I am thrilled for Aimee! Her hard work has paid off. Her success may not be visible in her bank account, but it's obvious looking at her smile. Her clients are healthier, and the women she hires from Alliance House are learning marketable skills they can apply anywhere.

"Where are you thinking about expanding?" I wonder if she'll open a center near Boston, or maybe close to Michael in Washington, DC.

"Actually, I was thinking about opening a second location in San Diego, near your center." I am shocked, and overjoyed.

"Really? You're thinking about coming out west?" I can't believe it. I was feeling sorry for myself, and now there is no reason for it at all!

"Remember our plans? We're all going to retire, live as neighbors and share the pool boy? Well, consider your move the first step. I'm next. I'll set up a second Wellness Clinic near you and once it is up and running, I'll retire from the day-to-day operations and stay on for consultation."

I am overjoyed! I will have a real friend living nearby. Regina was quick to jump in, "Joe and I expect to be retiring within a couple years. We love the mild winters of San Diego. I think after a couple more visits, I can convince him it's an ideal location for retirement."

I couldn't believe my ears! Aimee, then Regina. We're all going to be together again. In San Diego.

Lauren jumped in "Shamus and I won't be there for while. Paige isn't even in kindergarten yet. I guess nothing is stopping us from moving there now and having her grow up as a California girl." That would never happen. Shamus has been with the same company for most of his career. He'll be retiring from there when the time is right. They won't be coming soon, but it was nice of her to say they might.

Todd is in high school. Susan won't consider any move until he's in college. By then, maybe she and Bob will be married. Who knows?

Epilogue

All my life I thought 50 was so old. Your life is done. You might as well start looking for the perfect nursing home to settle into. I can't believe how wrong I was. In the past few years, there have been more doors opening for me, and more opportunities available. At this point in my life, I have the freedom and the means to jump at them.

The older we get, the more gusto we use when pursuing opportunities. The ride may be wild, but we hang on tight! Whether it's new found love, old loves cherished and deepened, or new ways to help others, we live our lives with passion.

The Posse isn't moving on without me. They're moving on and embracing me tightly within their circle. Act One might have taken fifty years, but Act Two was a short one. The curtains are going down. Hang on to your seat, it's time for Act Three!

Acknowledgements

First, I'd like to thank the Posse – Rosemarie Montuori, Trish Puntumapanitch, Beth Jacobsen, and Pamela Fraser. I don't know how I could survive without each one of you. You inspire me to be more than I ever thought possible. Thanks for the decades of experiences to draw from for this book! Let me apologize for giving the characters you inspired traits you do not have, nor would ever put up with! Remember, this is all fiction!

To all my girlfriends, not just the Posse, but the rest of you – Deborah Townsend, who lightened my load every day. Each night, as I sat down to write this novel, I could clear my mind because I knew Deborah was keeping things under control at work and had my back. She's my right hand man – ah, woman, and I couldn't have done this without her. And to Janet Bogle, who gave me a present every Friday while I was creating this novel. She has no idea how much pressure she puts me under every time she exclaims "You are my hero". I hope I can live up to her expectations.

To my Book Club Girlfriends, Suzette Jakielo, Leah Sawyer, Kim Donovan Borowski, Janet Bogle, Noreen Prescott, Elizabeth Grucelski, Beth Pietro, and Maryann Collins Tryon. You taught me how to enjoy reading books from all genres. More importantly, you taught me that every book has some redeeming qualities. Even if you don't like a book in its entirety, you can always find something you like about it. I hope you all find something you like in this book. Suzette, if we didn't bond over margaritas all those years ago, I may have never ambled down this path. You invited me to Book Club, which encouraged my love for reading to flourish.

To my family, who suffered through the long silences and frequent disappearances throughout the writing and editing processes. Funny how a coffee shop can be less distracting than a TV and a load of laundry.

And a final thanks to my cousins Lisa and Heather Wadley. When I asked "what have you been up to?" at Thanksgiving two years ago, you responded "writing a book". I never expecting the following year, I'd be answering the same way. Aspiring authors, check out NaNoWriMo.org for all the support, maybe even the nudge you need, to write your own book.

-B

ABOUT THE AUTHOR

Brenda Ann Fraser is a native of Massachusetts. She has moved from the small town of Weymouth, to the city of Worcester and finally the beaches of Cape Cod, where she and her family have lived for the past decade. She has always enjoyed reading as an escape from the pressure and doldrums of her career in the high tech industry.

Act Two is her first novel.

Made in the USA
Charleston, SC
13 October 2011